The
Unimportant Man

Jeremy Nichols

Published under Ceuta Publishing

First Edition

Published in the United States

ISBN: 061558442X
ISBN-13: 978-0615584423

About the Author

Jeremy Nichols is an author and filmmaker whose writing credits include the apologetic "On the Beauty of Christ and Christian Reason" and whose film credits include the supernatural (and controversial) motion picture about AIDS entitled THE AFRICAN CAMPAIGN - More information about THE AFRICAN CAMPAIGN is available at www.jerseynumbernine.co.uk

Praise for "On the Beauty of Christ and Christian Reason"

"A sincere and devout reading of the Christian revelation, and I think that the 'beautiful idea' approach might very well be as far as one can get, by explaining the power of Christianity to those who have not felt it."

Dr. Roger Scruton - Former lecturer and professor of aesthetics at Birkbeck College, London; former professor of philosophy and university professor, Boston University; and author of over 30 books, including Art and Imagination (1974), The Aesthetics of Music (1997), and A Political Philosophy: Arguments for Conservatism (2006).

Facebook:
"On the Beauty of Christ and Christian Reason"

"For we proclaimed before the Lord that he resembles a babe in arms, or a root in waterless soil; there is no trace of shapeliness or splendor about him. **We saw him, and he had neither comeliness nor beauty; his appearance was mean, and inferior to that of other men. He was familiar with hard labor and the lash, and schooled to endure weakness; for he kept his face averted, and was despised and disregarded.** Yet this is he who carries the burden of our sins, and suffers pain on our behalf. We took him for a man whose lot was toil and blows and indignities; but it was for our sins that he was wounded, and for our iniquities that he was afflicted. The chastisement that brought our peace fell upon him, and by his bruises we were healed. All of us went astray like sheep, each man taking his own wrong path; and for our sins the Lord delivered him up. Through all his ill-treatment he never opened his mouth; he was led away like a sheep to be slaughtered, and like a lamb that is mute before its shearer he never opened his lips. **His sentence was to be humiliated.**"

Clement of Rome (Pope Clement I)
The First Epistle of Clement to the Corinthians

"Be a sinner and sin boldly, but believe and rejoice in Christ even more boldly."

Martin Luther

PART I.

1.

The French film director, Jean-Luc Godard, said, "All you need to make a movie is a girl and a gun." By that, he likely meant that all you need to make a popular movie is sex and violence.

Godard's formula seems not just true for cinema. Most, if not all, entertainment appears to thrive on that combination.

Consider athletics, television, and mainstream fiction: Well-received sporting events have blood, sweat, and attractive celebrities in attendance (if not competing, as is the case nowadays with many comely and highly marketable professional athletes); television programs anticipate lengthy runs to the extent that they are overtly sexual and gratuitously violent (that is, "Too Hot for T.V."); and because mainstream fiction now aspires to be "A Major Motion Picture", the cinematic advice of Godard the *auteur* applies equally well to the craft of writing fictitious prose narratives: "All you need [to write a book] is a girl and a gun."

2.

With the gun barrel pressed into the back of his head, the pizza delivery man remembers Jean-Luc Godard's 1963 film, *Le Mepris*, starring Brigitte Bardot.

The pizza delivery man wants to compliment his assailant; he wants to tell her that (from what he glimpsed of her face) she looks like the French movie star as she appeared in the film's original promotional poster. However, because he also remembers that there is a time and a place for everything (and now is not likely the time), the pizza delivery man holds his tongue.

"Besides," he thinks, "I might be wrong. It happened so fast."

All of it happened so fast - The pizza delivery man's assailant (who might resemble Brigitte Bardot) stunned him when she drew the revolver from beneath the bed sheets; disarmed him when she ran naked at him from across the motel room; and disorientated him when she quickly spun him around, dropped him to his knees, pressed the revolver against the base of his skull, and inadvertently forced him to recollect a French actress of the New Wave.

Though barraged by intrusive and inquisitive thoughts, the pizza delivery man chooses to remain quiet: "No, I don't want to be wrong. Anyway, I should probably pay attention - She might want to fucking kill me."

3.

If you write a book about a pizza delivery man, then you are writing a comedy. Perhaps if the pizza delivery man is a struggling Bangladeshi immigrant with children to feed, then you might be writing a tragedy - But if the pizza delivery man is a born-and-raised national, then you are just a comedian.

Something about delivering pizzas deprives a man of the human right to be tragic.

Even though delivering pizzas is fundamentally the same as harvesting, Steinbeck would not write about the pizza delivery man.

The pizza delivery man is comedic. He is especially comedic when he dies on the job - The thought of a grown man shot while delivering pizza pies, breadsticks, and garlic dipping sauce tickles us.

4.

In her book, *A Cry in the Silence (2003)*, Brigitte Bardot wrote, "Our lovely, kind street-walkers have been replaced by girls from the East, Nigerians, travelers, transsexuals, drag-queens, bearers of AIDS and other friendly gifts... Not even French prostitutes are what they used to be."

For argument's sake, imagine that Old Madame Bardot speaks for France.

Now, imagine that Old Madame Bardot speaks for the entire West; which should be easy. Because of non-French authors like Henry Miller, the entire West might also look fondly on Old Madame Bardot's purported halcyon days of French whoring: The days when French whores were "lovely" and "kind".

Apart from misrepresenting past French prostitutes, Old Madame Bardot's xenophobic,

homophobic, and likely racist remarks do two things:
1) They deprive modern Nigerian street-walkers (and
others) the appellations "lovely" and "kind"; and 2)
They lay bare that peculiarity of Western social
stratification wherein French whores of the past
arguably rank higher than today's pizza delivery
men.

Though French whores of the past absolutely
spread their own "friendly gifts", spread shame, and
distressed marriages and families; in the West, they
are "lovely" and "kind".

Because loveliness and kindness are qualities
that ennoble suffering and engender empathy; in the
West (at least in retrospect), past French whores can
be tragic.

Because pizza delivery men cannot be tragic,
they exist in our Western hierarchy tiers below the
past French hookers with "hearts of gold".

If we believe that Old Madame Bardot speaks
for the West, then pizza delivery men reside in our
social consciousness alongside those she believes
cannot be "lovely" and "kind": Disenfranchised

sexual minorities, carriers of contagions, and
foreigners.

In that sense, in the company of foreigners,
delivering pizzas exiles a man. When a man rings the
first customer's doorbell (caters the first slumber
party) he forfeits his citizenship - He becomes an
oddity: The native-foreigner.

Re-imagine Socrates: Was he asked to choose
between hemlock and delivering pizzas?

Rightly, it is wrong to imagine that Old
Madame Bardot speaks for all of France and the West
when she discusses modern whores - Nigerian street-
walkers (and others) can be "lovely" and "kind".
However, it is not wrong to imagine that Old
Madame Bardot might speak for the West when she
paints a romantic and over-sentimental portrait of
past French whores. Her poor study of the Gallic
prostitute from the past is arguably a part of our
Western mythos - Accepting this, the inconspicuous
absence of a man, his pizza pies, and his six-pack of
soda in our western mythography still amounts to his
psychic exile.

5.

The woman who might look like the young Brigitte Bardot has a steady hand.

The pizza delivery man does not notice that because he is searching the room for a reflective surface by which he can see her face - The pizza delivery man wants to confirm his suspicion.

Because he must be cautious; because he cannot move his head (for fear he might startle her, forcing her to fire); because there are no reflective surfaces within his immediate eye-sight, the pizza delivery man is unsuccessful.

Disappointed, he thinks, "Pizza delivery men don't carry more than $20. As a result, we're, generally, killed for three reasons: 1) A little bit of money; 2) For kicks; or 3) A combination of a little bit of money and kicks.

"Because my attacker hasn't asked for money, I can't convince her that $20 isn't worth the trouble. Because my attacker hasn't asked for money, she's doing this for the thrill. Because she's doing this for the thrill, I can't appeal to her goddamn reason."

The pizza delivery man recognizes that thrill-seekers see the world differently – In that respect, thrill-seekers are like him.

6.

The pizza delivery man is a synesthete - He has Grapheme-color synesthesia: A psychological condition from which he neither suffers nor benefits.

When a man with Grapheme-color synesthesia sees, hears, or thinks about a particular number, letter or letter combination; when he experiences a grapheme, he sees a color.

For instance, when the pizza delivery man thinks about the $20 maximum he is permitted to carry by his corporate pizzeria, he sees the color pink: The color of a piglet.

7.

Squirming, the pizza delivery man feels like a stuck pig.

He feels like a terminal patient.

Inwardly, he asks himself: "If a man has an appointment with death (as I seem to have right now), is that man dying?"

Unintentionally aloud, he then asks himself, "Is getting closer to my death like becoming sicker?"

"Madame Bardot" does not understand her intended victim: "What the fuck did you just say?"

8.

Before she phoned for the extra large, hand-tossed pizza with pepperonis, black olives, and green peppers, "Madame Bardot" thought about the murder of a pizza delivery man.

"If I kill a pizza boy (who'll likely be a man)," she conjectured, "not one news program will report his death as a tragic loss. After all, a dead pizza boy isn't like a dead John F. Kennedy Jr."

She thought about the local media and what they would say: "If I kill a pizza boy, the local media will talk about the world in which we live; the deaths of pizza boys spark debates about larger social ills."

It seemed to "Madame Bardot" that the real tragedy of a murdered pizza boy was the murderer's fall from grace, and "Madame Bardot" has always wanted to be a tragedienne.

9.

Before she placed her order, "Madame Bardot" also thought about the people in the pizza delivery man's life: Those who would personally know him.

Because she does not believe that pizza delivery men have "true friends of substance", she seriously considered only one conceivable person in a pizza delivery man's life: His mother.

"Madame Bardot" considered the pizza delivery man's mother because she was a legitimate obstacle between her and a murderous thrill.

Fortunately for "Madame Bardot's" murderous urge, she concluded, "Surely, the lament of the pizza boy's mother will be for the promise her son might once have shown, for the man he might once have been."

When she imagined the pizza delivery man's mother, "Madame Bardot" saw a woman weeping for the son she never actually had. She envisioned the police knocking on that woman's front-door to return her son's bright, flour-coated, blood-splattered corporate uniform - "Madame Bardot" imagined a disappointed woman, saddened that the uniform was not a neatly folded flag.

10.

"What the fuck did you say?"

The pizza delivery man says, "Nothing."

"Madame Bardot" strikes the back of his skull with the butt of her revolver.

"Madame Bardot" struck the pizza delivery man because she wants to know the truth - She also struck him because lies offend her.

"Madame Bardot" has principles.

She knows that what she is doing is wrong; that is why she chose a pizza delivery man - Killing a pizza delivery man is less wrong.

Killing a pizza delivery man does not force spectators at a sporting event to observe a moment of silence - It does not inconvenience anyone that much.

"Madame Bardot" asks again: "What the fuck did you say?"

Now, the pizza delivery man has an unbearable headache. He cannot think clearly.

He tells "Madame Bardot" that he cannot remember: "Because you fucking hit me, that's why."

"Madame Bardot" accepts that.

She tells him to take a minute: "But remember."

Eventually, the pizza delivery man does: "Is getting closer to my death like becoming sicker?"

"Madame Bardot" asks the pizza delivery man to explain.

Because few people ask him to explain, she flatters him.

"Because you're likely going to kill me, I have an appointment with death. Because the appointment draws nearer with every fucking second, am I like an incurable cancer patient growing more unwell?"

Still, "Madame Bardot" does not understand.

The pizza delivery man continues: "I don't expect you to tell me, but I wonder if I look worse than when I knocked on your motel door. Sure, I look like shit, but I wonder if I look like I have become more ill. I thought I was healthy-"

The pizza delivery man wrings his hands.

"But here you are (like the French Marilyn Monroe) showing me that I'm actually very unhealthy. I feel sick. I feel that I'm becoming sicker. And when you pull that trigger, then I'll be the sickest I've ever been."

The pizza delivery man pauses, and then adds, "You're like a fucking tumor in my lungs, and I wonder how I could have prevented you - I wonder what grew you in me."

"Madame Bardot" is angry with herself: "Why am I listening to you? You're *just* a pizza boy."

11.

The most powerful word in the English language is not "No".

Most victims of sexual assault likely screamed "No" and still became victims.

Which is not to say that there is a single English word that can prevent a rape, but there is a word that might (in the right context) rape the rapist.

That word is "Just": The most powerful word in the English language: A powerfully delimiting word that has the potential to assault a man's dignity: That English word which can rape a man.

Because sexual assaults are often power struggles, an English-speaking woman might turn the power-dynamic on its head with the following utterance: "You're *just* a/an [contemptuous word or expression] who can't [a typically/stereotypically male function], so you rape!"

To further illustrate the awesome power of "Just", imagine the following three successful men in domestic arguments: David Beckham, Brad Pitt, and Barack Obama.

To submit her "Golden Balls", Victoria Beckham might only need to tell her husband, "You're *just* a footballer, David – You're hardly Hollywood royalty."

Likewise, Angelina Jolie might only need to remind her significant other that he is *just* an actor: "Hardly the President of the United States of America."

Though First Lady Michelle Obama seems to have the more difficult challenge, her husband might also succumb to the most powerful word in the English language: "You're *just* a politician, Barack, with (at best) an eight year shelf life - You're not a Roman Emperor."

Of course, "Just" could only strip those men of dignity if they did not avail themselves of the defense to which all men of accomplishment have recourse.

12.

When Julius Caesar died (the victim of multiple senatorial penetrations); as he lay sprawled in a pool of his own blood, he still reached for his *toga picta*; brought it to his face; and shielded his offended dignity.

Originally, the *toga picta* (an all-purple toga with gold-thread embroidery) was worn by Roman generals during their after-war processions: Their Triumphs. It was Julius Caesar, the dandy, who first wore it regularly. For Caesar, the *toga picta* distinguished him from lesser men - It proclaimed him first among equals.

Today, successful men do not wear *toga pictas* (or anything of the kind, really – Chief Executive

Officers wear the tired Beau Brummell suit and tie like everyone else). Lacking twenty feet of purple wool draped around their bodies; when assaulted, successful modern men must reach for something else to guard their honor, assert their worth.

Nowadays, because of rampant and hollow egalitarianism, the accomplished man attacked with the word "Just", if he so chooses (and he usually does), reaches for the head of a lesser man – Which he delivers like a sacrifice to the offending woman: "See, at least I don't deliver pizzas – Those guys suck balls!"

Note: Ancient Romans denied foreigners the right to wear the toga.

13.

"Madame Bardot" verbally assaulted the pizza delivery man when she asked herself aloud, "Why am I listening to you? You're *just* a pizza boy."

Because he has long been the "lowest man on the totem pole"; because people regularly strip him down with words, the attack was nothing new for the pizza delivery man.

The only thing new was his response - He winced.

When "Madame Bardot" struck him with the word "Just", the pizza delivery man flinched for the first time in a very, very long time.

Stunned, he wondered: "Did I recoil from pain or fear?"

Though ignorant about the cause of his startled withdrawal, the pizza delivery man knew well enough that he wanted to remove his pizza delivery man's flour-encrusted, logo-embossed, coordinating baseball cap; lower it to his face; and cover his curiously shamed expression as if such a thing had never happened before.

14.

Hesitation happens when people doubt. People hesitate because they want or need more time to consider what they were about to do.

Hesitation says, "Upon further investigation, you will better know the correctness of an action."

Hesitation promises reassurance one way or another, but it does not always deliver – Sometimes it directly commits us to our original course or restrains us in no uncertain terms, while other times it is simply a prelude to tentative activity or inaction.

At this moment, "Madame Bardot" hesitates.

She hesitates because she wants to pull the trigger with confidence. She hesitates because a thought entered her mind around the time the pizza delivery man winced, and she is now ill-at-ease.

She looks to hesitation to help her regain what she has lost.

Unfortunately for her, "Madame Bardot" knows that hesitation does not always validate the original course. Because of that, she also fears - She fears its (emphatic or otherwise) resistance to the murder of the pizza delivery man.

Hesitation compounds the distress that made her hesitate.

"God Damnit!" she curses.

The pizza delivery man braces himself.

Hesitation is like a judge presiding over "Madame Bardot's" perversion; and she desperately needs a favorable decision. She does not want a nagging thought to interfere with the enjoyment of her thrill. She imagines killing someone is like excellent sex and few things are worse for her than a distracted mind during intercourse.

"Madame Bardot" wants to live in the moment.

Consider the following: It is difficult for her to orgasm if she thinks that she left the car window down on a night when it is likely to rain. On a night when it might rain, "Madame Bardot" (for the sake of her sexual fulfillment) must make sure she has not overlooked anything.

For "Madame Bardot", the moral problem of killing a pizza delivery man for kicks is solved as easily as checking on a car window that might be open a smidge.

15.

"You're just a pizza boy, right?"

Because conscience makes us cowards, "Madame Bardot" trembles slightly.

She repeats, and then rephrases her question: "You're just a fucking pizza boy, right? I mean, you're not someone important? Or someone who will be important, right?"

The pizza delivery man knows that his life depends on his response. He knows the convention: When asked about their work, pizza delivery men must answer, "I deliver pizzas, but I'm really…"

All pizza delivery men work at least two jobs. The pizza delivery man's second job (should he have no other) is to explain how delivering pizzas is just a step towards something better: A more respectable profession with greater earning potential.

Put another way, being a pizza delivery man is like being that defendant tried over-and-over for the same crime: Being without grander aspirations.
16.

In Ancient Rome, the *homo sacer* (or "sacred man") was a man denied all civil rights.

In his book, ***Homo Sacer: Sovereign Power and Bare Life (1998)***, Italian philosopher, Giorgio Agamben, used the *homo sacer* to illustrate the following point: When the State denies a man his civil rights then it denies him his supposedly natural and inalienable rights (such as the right to life).

Although the *homo sacer* remained biologically a man, without his civil rights, he was no longer a man in the political sense – According to the principle (that is, according to the law), the *homo sacer* could be killed by anyone.

In the Cincius Alimentus and Calpurnius Piso telling, the Roman Senate branded Spurius Maelius as a *homo sacer* to strip him of the civil right to due process, and then murdered him without a trial.

Because "Madame Bardot" is a principled woman; for her conscience, she does not need to prove that the pizza delivery man is guilty of anything like a real crime. She only needs to prove that he is a modern-day *homo sacer*: A non-citizen: A foreigner in her midst: A pizza delivery man.

When she does that, then she can kill him "execution-style" for a laugh.

17.

If a man tells you that he delivers pizzas for a living and does not follow this with an apology ("But

I'm really..."), then he drives you to do one of two things. Either he makes you lie, forcing you to say stupid and unbelievable things like "That must be rewarding!" and "You're like your own boss! Sometimes I think about selling my practice and just delivering pizzas!" or he makes you tell the truth.

You can express that truth in either word or deed (and, of course, a combination of the two).

If you communicate the truth by deed; if you express truth by action, then you might choose to walk away from the pizza delivery man who does not aspire to something else or you might choose to hang around and glower.

If you are "Madame Bardot", then putting a bullet through the pizza delivery man's brain is acceptable, too.

If you prefer words, then you must choose again: Between the subtle and the overt.

Because subtlety thrives on ambiguity, you might address the offending pizza delivery man like this: "I bet the adult films got it right - Housewives must really want to fuck a pizza boy."

If you are overt, then you just need to tell the pizza delivery man that you consider him unworthy of serious consideration – In a word, you just need to call him frivolous.

18.

In the West, the Ancient Romans cast out the *homo sacer*; and though the *homo sacer* was a uniquely Western state-of-being, the East has also had its own outcasts (or Untouchables). Famously, there have been the *Dalit* of India and Nepal; the *Burakumin* of Japan; and the *Baekjeong* of Korea.

Before the Mongolian hordes arrived on the Korean peninsula, Koreans divided their outcasts into two groups: The *Hwachae* and the *Jaein*. The *Hwachae* (or *Suchae*) were those deemed contaminated by their trade (men such as butchers). The *Jaein*, however – The performers and prostitutes of pre-Mongol Korea – were cast out because an austere Korean culture judged them to be unworthy of serious consideration.

Sober Koreans dismissed the *Jaein* as frivolous.

19.

"Madame Bardot" whispers into the ear of the pizza delivery man.

"Answer me," she says.

Her naked left nipple brushes against the nape of the pizza delivery man's neck: "Are you or are you not an important man?"

The pizza delivery man says nothing.

A memory distracts him – He remembers the last time a naked woman whispered into his ear - It was at that useless fucking college.

Earlier, the woman and the pizza delivery man had had sex. She later confessed that her heart was not in it.

Because she was high and ordinarily inconsiderate, she also confessed to admiring their statistics professor: "[Pizza delivery man], have you ever met a man so intelligent that he humbled you?"

Because the pizza delivery man had too often met men like that, he grumbled, "So?" and then looked at his bedside clock – He did not want to be late for his first night as a part-time pizza delivery man.

Draping her arm across his still-hairless chest, the last naked woman to whisper in his ear asked the pizza delivery man about his plans for the future.

Because he resented unfair comparisons to their statistics professor (and other titled men), the pizza delivery man pushed the woman aside; reached for a joint; rolled back onto the bed; and told the woman (who had now covered her breasts) that she sounded like she wanted a man with more talent.

Hurt that she had been thrust aside, the woman replied that she certainly wanted a man with "Something".

The pizza delivery man remembers attacking her: "Your talented statistician wants one thing and one thing only!"

Because she had not consciously considered their statistics professor as a man interested in her; because her response was not properly ruminated; because it had not passed through her, admittedly poor, censoring filters; because she spat it out before she had had time to digest it and its implications, it was brutally honest: "Some things are worth that price, [Pizza delivery man]!"

He remembers calling her a whore.

To which the last naked woman who whispered in his ear said, "There are worse things to be."

At the time, the pizza delivery man did not know she was talking about him.

20.

When he was a boy, grown-ups told the pizza delivery man, "Everyone has a talent: Something that they do better than others."

Because the young pizza delivery man had no recognizable talent; because that shortcoming troubled him, the young pizza delivery man found the grown-ups' words very reassuring.

They helped him sleep.

At night, he would drift off fantasizing about his dormant gift. Because he enjoyed music, he often wished he would wake the next morning with a better ear: "Please, God" he would pray, "perfect pitch?"

As the years passed, the still talentless pizza delivery man became restless.

"When will I find my talent?" he would ask.

Because he was still a boy, grown-ups continued to ply his heart with optimism: "Give yourself time," they would say. "However modest, you will find something uniquely yours, something for which you will feel pride."

Because he was still young, the grown-ups' words comforted him.

Unfortunately, the pizza delivery man could not stay young forever.

As he aged, the grown-ups' reassuring words grew fewer and farther between, until one day they stopped. The adults who once insisted that everything was going to be alright (that his talent would reveal itself in time) now demanded that the talentless pizza delivery man get with the program; work with what he had; and face the music that he could not make.

As a grown-up, nighttime became something different for the pizza delivery man. Because he will never wake with anything like a well-tuned ear, nighttime is no longer a time for fantasy. It is now just that time (after fitful tossing and turning) when the pizza delivery man resigns himself to the fact that he has nothing of which to be proud.

Raised in a society that celebrates musicians, performers, athletes, models, published writers, intellects, entrepreneurs, charismatic statesmen, and other talented people; having long believed that talent is the standard against which a man's importance is measured, nighttime is now just that time when the pizza delivery man sees most clearly that he is an unimportant man.

21.

The pizza delivery man shudders: "I am an important man."

Were "Madame Bardot" a betting woman, then she would have called the pizza delivery man's lie. She did not expect him to say, "I am an important man, and here is the proof." Neither did she expect a suicidal admission of unimportance or silence, which is almost tantamount to a confession of insignificance.

Because the pizza delivery man has not volunteered evidence, "Madame Bardot" remarks that he could not have said anything else: "After all, your life depends on that lie."

Desperately, the pizza delivery man wants to challenge her (even though he has not thought far enough ahead and created an acceptable alter-ego): "I'm not fucking lying!"

Digging the revolver into the base of his skull, "Madame Bardot" reasserts the power-dynamic: "Then tell me, potty mouth liar – Who are you, really?"

The pizza delivery man clenches his fists. Furiously, his mind searches for a plausible state-of-being that will save his life.

For a split-second, he wonders if he should pretend to be a medical student. He does not because "Madame Bardot" would never believe him. He knows that she would question him about the human body, and he would not have the answer.

The pizza delivery man panics because he faces a similar problem with each potentially assumed identity – He knows that he cannot rise to her challenges.

"If I claim to be an architect or a classical composer," he thinks, "she'll insist that I sketch or compose something; and then I'll be fucked."

The pizza delivery man knows that he is condemned because he cannot be someone else.

He feels a lump in his dry throat - He believes he feels a tumor metastasizing somewhere inside him.

Impatient with the pizza delivery man's reticence, "Madame Bardot" withdraws the revolver's muzzle from the rolls of scrunched flesh on the pizza delivery man's neck.

She takes several steps backward.

Terrified that "Madame Bardot" is set to pull the trigger, the pizza delivery man further rounds his shoulders, trying to shield his exposed head like a turtle.

Inwardly, he screams, "My God, this is it!"

His entire body tenses, bracing for the end, tendons absurdly taut before the inevitable limpness when he falls like a marionette cut loose.

Click!

The pizza delivery man's body jolts. It jerks and shivers spasmodically. Like an asthmatic (or fish out of water), he fights for air. When he manages one shallow breath, he smells the smoke circulated through the motel room by the air-conditioning vents. When he manages the second (and unexpected inhalation), he is surprised to discover that gunpowder smells like tobacco smoke.

"Madame Bardot" laughs: "Fucking hell, pizza boy – Don't give yourself a heart attack."

22.

"Madame Bardot" takes a drag on her cigarette.

For effect, she opens and closes her silver lighter: "Click. Click. Click."

Momentarily, the pizza delivery man is relieved to be alive, but the sense of relief quickly fades when he considers that nothing has changed.

Distracted by his thoughts, the pizza delivery man startles when "Madame Bardot" reaches over his shoulder and drops a "Thank you for not smoking" sign into his lap.

She wonders aloud if the motel will later display "Thank you for not shooting pizza boys" signs.

Dropping ash on the pizza delivery man's head, "Madame Bardot" chortles: "Really, who dreams this shit up?"

Her chortle is familiar - It sets the pizza delivery man's mind into motion.

He thinks that he knows "Madame Bardot", but he cannot remember from where.

Examining his assailant's peculiar laugh, he thinks, "She is a grown woman who snorts through her nose like a pig and chuckles like a simpleton."

The pizza delivery man searches his memory for a woman who obnoxiously snorts like a pig and chuckles like a simpleton.

Unable to recall such a woman, the pizza delivery man curses himself, and then notices the "Thank you for not smoking sign" in his lap – A single piece of bent red plastic with a noticeably high gloss.

Because "Madame Bardot" has once more taken several steps back, the pizza delivery man has just enough unobserved space to balance the sign on his knee without arousing suspicion. Adjusting it slightly; using its reflective surface like a hand-mirror, the pizza delivery man is finally able to confirm his two suspicions regarding "Madame Bardot": Firstly, "Madame Bardot" does indeed look like a young French actress of the New Wave (though not so pretty); and secondly, the pizza delivery man does know her - "Madame Bardot" has a face which most everyone in the country would recognize.

23.

With a cigarette dangling from her lips; with one hand pointing the revolver at the pizza delivery man's back, "Madame Bardot" scrolls through her cell phone's text messages. Alerted to an incoming call by her personalized ring-tone (a song by a popular Haitian-American musician), she contorts her face and declines it.

Somewhat star-struck, the pizza delivery man continues to watch "Madame Bardot" in the reflection of the "Thank you for not smoking" sign. It is like he is at home, watching her on the television as he is accustomed.

When she chortles again because something she has read is funny, the pizza delivery man (like a distant viewing audience member) disapproves of her callousness.

"How did this talentless bitch get her own show?" he quietly asks himself

24.

Sitting in the parking lot of "Madame Bardot's" motel, Robin Fletcher rolls down his car window and fumbles with his first pack of herbal cigarettes.

Fuming, he replays an argument his ex-wife and he had had several weeks ago.

It began when she mentioned their son: "And his anti-social ways."

Fletcher grimaces when he remembers that he had only asked his ex-wife to be more specific.

She tutted, "Don't you know anything about your son?"

Fletcher responded that he knew a lot: "And more, because he tells me things that he doesn't tell you."

He thinks about how satisfied he was when his ex-wife demanded to know what their son had told only him.

Fletcher answered that he could not say: "Because he trusted me not to tell, that's why" – Even though his son had made no such condition.

His ex-wife had wanted to say, "You're his father, not his friend, Robin," but stopped herself because that was another argument. Instead, she stayed the course: "Do you know what a blog is, Robin?"

Fletcher hates when his ex-wife says his name.

Through gritted teeth, he answered, "Yes, I know what a blog is, [My ex-wife]."

"Well, your son does nothing but write them. He never leaves his room. He just sits in front of his computer, shooting blogs into cyberspace-"

Befuddled (and concerned that his son might be embroiled in something perverse), Fletcher interrupted his ex-wife: "What's he writing about?"

Fletcher's ex-wife smirked, and then snidely replied, "Oh, don't you know? He thinks he's in show business like his father – He's writing gossip columns."

Displeased that his wife had punctuated the phrase "show business" with condescending hand gestures; finding nothing wrong with his son aspiring to be a columnist, Fletcher firmly stated his opinion: "There's nothing wrong with the boy's interest in journalism, [My ex-wife]."

Robin Fletcher's ex-wife hates it when he says her name.

"He doesn't want to be a journalist, Robin!"

Fletcher shouted that he wanted to know how she knew that: "How is it you're so goddamn sure?"

To which his ex-wife snapped back, "Because he's your son! He doesn't care about journalism – He just cares about celebrity coat-tails and riding them to fame!"

Fletcher demanded that she wait ("One fucking second!"), but his ex-wife would not.

"Nobody reads blogs, Robin! There aren't enough people on this earth to read all of the shit that's on the internet!"

Before Fletcher could tell his ex-wife just how many "hits" his site receives in a week, she changed tactic and spoke imploringly: "Please, our son cannot end up just another struggling *paparazzo*."

Insulted, Fletcher asked his ex-wife what she would rather their son become.

She might have answered, but at that moment the boy arrived home from school.

25.

The word *paparazzo* comes from the Italian film, **La Dolce Vita** – A famous Fellini production starring Marcello Mastroianni. In the film, the actor, Walter Santesso, plays a news photographer so named.

According to a possibly apocryphal story, Fellini chose the name Paparazzo because in an Italian dialect with which he was familiar *paparazzo* meant mosquito (or the annoying buzz of a mosquito).

In that light, it is understandable that Robin Fletcher took offence when his ex-wife called him a *paparazzo* – Naturally, Fletcher does not want to be a mosquito (even if only by association).

When he was a boy, Robin Fletcher did not tell his classmates, "When I grow up, I want to be a disease-spreading insect."

When he was a boy (like most boys, if not all), Fletcher wanted to be one thing: Biologically and politically a man: A complete man.

Though he has attained biological manhood (A feat likely achieved with his first pubic hair, sexual encounter, or the birth of his son), Robin Fletcher still has not fulfilled his youthful aspiration to be politically a man.

Fletcher, like many men, has found it far easier to grow "short-and-curlies" than to achieve relevance in a world strewn with words like "Just" and "*Paparazzo*".

In such a hostile environment, men like Robin Fletcher find their self-identifications knocked from their persons and replaced by more invidious designations. Where Fletcher would prefer the honorable distinction photojournalist, ex-wives and others, like totalitarian thugs, affix *paparazzo* – Which feels so much like a pink triangle: An emasculation.

Repeatedly, people call Robin Fletcher a *paparazzo*, and repeatedly he must fight to convince them of the skills required by his trade and of the higher purpose (that is, the politically relevant man's requisite noble aim) it serves.

"Do you want your kids looking up to frauds?" he asks. "The truth, even if it is about celebrities (who I might add possess awesome soft power) is never vulgar and pointless."

Often, Fletcher adds, "If it were up to me, we'd all live in glass houses like the commies wanted."

26.

Though Frank Lloyd Wright took issue with his "un-American style", the German-born architect,

Mies van der Rohe, was not a communist. In 1946, when he designed the glass-walled Farnsworth House for Illinois nephrologist, Edith Farnsworth, he was a capitalist.

Philip Johnson, the American-born architect and apologetic former Nazi-sympathizer (again, not a communist), copied Mies' glass house design for his own residence in New Canaan, Connecticut.

Johnson liked the 360 degree landscape views: The mutable "wallpaper".

From the inside looking out, glass homes with ever-changing "wallpaper" do seem ideal. However, from the outside looking in, glass homes with glass walls present a serious problem for most home buyers – The neighbors can see you shit.

Mies believed he had solved the problem.

He called his solution the "core": An enclosure in the home for private areas like toilets, showers, and mechanical elements.

Unfortunately, Mies did not solve the entire problem. Though people cannot see you shit while you are in the private enclosure, they can still see how often you shit ("There's Old Edith Farnsworth back in the toilet, again! That bitch needs to stop eating Thai Green Curry.")

Although everyone shits (and it is no great embarrassment for most to enter a public restroom), everyone shits with different regularity.

For those who shit embarrassingly infrequently or frequently; for those on either side of the Defecating Bell Curve, glass houses are nightmares.

27.

Even when they camp-out for a weekend in a seedy motel room, celebrities like "Madame Bardot" live in glass houses.

When celebrities enter a normal room with opaque walls, they turn these walls into partitions for their "core".

Because they always have a "core", celebrities always have a private area that is fodder for speculation. Though the *paparazzi* cannot often see inside it, they always know enough to write page after page of sensational gossip – *Paparazzi* know that private things happen inside private spaces.

Because the pizza delivery man is right now inside "Madame Bardot's" "core", he is (in the words of Robin Fletcher) part of her "fair game" personal life.

As we are more the company that we keep in private than simply the company we keep, Robin Fletcher sits in his car, observing and wondering, "What the hell is [Madame Bardot] doing with this guy? Is she going to throw everything away to fuck a pizza boy?"

28.

Although "Madame Bardot" wants to kill the pizza delivery man behind closed doors, she has known that nothing she could do behind closed doors with a pizza delivery man could stay that way.

"Madame Bardot" has known her entire privileged life that the *paparazzi* are always outside, stalking her.

Even if the pizza delivery man were capable of convincing her that he was someone more important,

"Madame Bardot" has known that he would have to convince the world, too – And having waited so long for the pizza delivery man's answer, she strongly disbelieves he can do that.

She growls, "Unfucking-believable!" before she brings the full weight of her predicament to bear down on the pizza delivery man's shoulders: "You'll have to be someone like Peter the Great, if I'm gonna spare you. You're going to have to be as impressive as a Russian tsar masquerading as a western commoner because I can't let those bastard *paparazzi* think I've sucked off a pizza boy!"

29.

Internally, "Madame Bardot" reminds herself that she knew the consequences when she placed the order for the extra large, hand-tossed pizza with pepperonis, black olives, and green peppers: "[Madame Bardot], you knew that when you let him in, you'd have to kill him and turn yourself over."

Staring down at the back of the pizza delivery man's head that drips with sweat, she feels like a Japanese soldier forced to adhere to a version of the

Bushido code of death before dishonor - For "Madame Bardot" (and the public to whom she caters), for whom the greatest scandal is to love (or seem to love) a lesser man, the pizza delivery man must die before she is disgraced.

Accepting the inexorable course of her actions, she is able to relax.

30.

On principle, "Madame Bardot" refuses to ask again.

"If I ask again," she thinks, "he'll suspect that I'm stalling. He'll think that I'm reluctant to do something that I obviously want to do. Already, he likely questions my resolve – Does this fucking pizza boy think that I lack will power?"

Because it is (as it has always been) important to "Madame Bardot" that she is perceived well, she tells the pizza delivery man that she is going to kill him now: "I've done the math. I don't believe that you've done important things, and I don't expect important things to come from you."

Choking on the urgency, the pizza delivery man spits out, "Wait, [Madame Bardot]! Christ, please wait! Yes, I deliver pizzas, but..."

"Madame Bardot" waits for just a moment, and then asks if a cat has got the pizza delivery man's tongue: "Or are you buying yourself more time to think of another lie, you faggot?"

31.

Mistakenly, most people believe that the truth is simple and easily expressed. They afford lies more time to incubate because they incorrectly think that only lies come from the imagination.

For hypocritical people like "Madame Bardot", only dishonest men hesitate.

Because the truth also relies on the imagination of the speaker to articulate it well, it is wrong not to give the truth time - It is unfair not to give the truth-teller air to breathe.

Like wine, the truth is best when decanted. Otherwise, the full flavor can be lost.

Of course, there are moments (such as now) when the full truth emerges prematurely and unexpectedly when the decanter is hoisted from the table-top and waved about by a belligerent drunk who threatens to shatter the innocent vessel against the wall.

32.

Like a glass decanter swung around, the pizza delivery man feels the dizzying effects of aeration – Truth's full flavor sparks his taste-buds and ignites his brain's synapses.

Whirling in the clutches of "Madame Bardot's" brazen perversion, the pizza delivery man keenly observes truth for the first time: "I feel like I've been kicked in the head by a mule."

By that, the pizza delivery man means that he feels like he has emerged from a freak accident with phenomenal mental acuity.

"Madame Bardot" demands that the pizza delivery man repeat himself.

Staring into the "Thank you for not smoking" sign perched on his knee; confronting "Madame Bardot" eye-to-eye for the first time, the pizza delivery man wants to repeat himself and more – He wants to communicate the truth which he now finds utterly intoxicating (and with full veracity).

He wants to explain that he was wrong to believe that being talentless equated to worthlessness - After all, "Madame Bardot" has no real talent.

The pizza delivery man wants to tell "Madame Bardot" about the last naked woman who whispered in his ear. He wants to tell "Madame Bardot" that he misunderstood when she said that she wanted a man with "Something". The pizza delivery man wants to confess that he mistakenly thought "Something" was a talent like the intellect of a statistics professor. He wants to clear the air about that - It might be something with larger parameters.

The pizza delivery man wants to tell "Madame Bardot" that he was not lying when he said that he was an important man – He might have that "Something", too.

He might actually have an important man inside him, and if "Madame Bardot" would only put down the gun, then he could find him for her (or even make him).

The pizza delivery man wants to add that when he does find or make that important man with "Something", then she (and the entire West) will acknowledge his citizenship; restore his civil rights; reintegrate him into the community from which he was cast out during adolescence; honor his political capacities; and finally recognize his worth.

33.

The pizza delivery man would communicate all of that were the pathway between his thoughts and mouth not twisted in fear, rendering him incapable of expressing more than "I feel like I've been kicked in the head by a mule."

With his thoughts trapped inside an inarticulate body, the pizza delivery man spasms as "Madame Bardot" passes sentence: "You're *just* a pizza boy."

Shivering uncontrollably, like a man retrieved from a glacial lake, the pizza delivery man sputters, "Please. Please, [Madame Bardot]."

But his begging is counter-productive - It only steels his executioner's resolve.

Promising to remember his last words (as best as she can), "Madame Bardot" asks the pizza delivery man if there is anything else he would like to say: "Other than you feel like a mule?"

Bound in a fear-induced paroxysm of convulsions, the pizza delivery man's eyes widen at this final affront, while a thickly Haitian-accented ring-tone blares in the background.

Wanting so badly to be understood (to assure "Madame Bardot" that he does not feel like a mule, but rather like a man who has been kicked in the head by a mule), the pizza delivery man does not pause to consider the consequences of barking, "No!"
34.

Robin Fletcher panics: "Holy shit! He's fucking shot her!"

He scrambles for his camera.

It does not occur to Fletcher that the pizza delivery man is the one whose brains are splattered against the motel wall. In Robin Fletcher's world, pizza delivery men are desperate and unprincipled animals: Just biologically men.

Rummaging through his rucksack for an appropriate lens, Fletcher suddenly stops – Only now does he appreciate that he just heard a real gunshot.

Nervously, he pulls at his thinning hair.

"Christ," he thinks, "I might have to save [Madame Bardot]."

Though Fletcher has always wanted to be a hero, he has never wanted to act heroically. He appreciates that things do not always go well for men who act heroically ("The best laid plans of mice and men.").

Not wanting to be shot for a coddled heiress, Fletcher considers driving away, but stops when he thinks of his ex-wife: "Wouldn't she just fucking love this!"

Incensed by the prospect of his ex-wife denouncing him for cowardice, Robin Fletcher rejects the option to flee.

Instead, he tells himself, "A man's gotta do what a man's gotta do." – Which, though a fitting response for another, is not completely appropriate for Robin Fletcher.

Although Robin Fletcher proclaims himself to be a fully incorporated citizen; although he fights tooth-and-nail for the title photojournalis*t*, he has not quite attained that state of being a whole man; that state from which manly feats are expected - For a man like Robin Fletcher, there is nothing that he must do simply because it is something that he must do.

Right now, he would be more honest with himself were he repeating, "If I am going to be a man, then I gotta do what a man's gotta do." – Even though that too is dishonest.

In his too-often enflamed bowels, Robin Fletcher actually suspects that, as far as the world is concerned, he is essentially not a man. For that, he strongly doubts there is a single deed that when performed could confer manhood upon him.

Believing that any act of heroism on his part will be attributed to an aberration, rather than a state of overlooked (or newly acquired) manliness; Robin Fletcher prepares himself for "Madame Bardot's" defense simply to assuage his ex-wife.

Doing up his pant zipper, he feels like a fraud.

35.

Consider the push-cart vendor who foils a robbery by shoving his cart into the criminal's path. Generally, the vendor's response to the enquiring media is that he did what any man would have done; which, when taken at face value, seems a very decent thing to say.

However, when more closely examined, the push-cart vendor's seemingly humble words actually reveal a cleverly scheming mind trying to insinuate itself into the citizenry with lies - He might just as well have said, "I did what any man would have done, ergo I am (as I have always been) a man – And shame on you all for treating me otherwise!" – Which is deceit in two respects: Firstly, the push-cart vendor has not always been a man (that is, he has not always been politically recognized); after all, he was serving *real* men from a push-cart; and secondly, because he was not a real man at the time of his so-called "heroic" deed, he could not have been compelled by the expectation to do what a man's gotta do – It would be like saying, "Because people believed I was a Lemur monkey, I climbed to the top of the tallest tree I could find."

No one expected the push-cart vendor to live-up to the expectations of a man (not even himself).

In truth, the push-cart vendor performed "heroically" only in order to become a man, not to realize the man he already was; and, in so doing, he made it impossible for those around him to see anything other than his off-putting egoism at work.

If he is lucky enough, the push-cart vendor is left to be an "Unsung Hero". Typically, however, savvy civil officials and journalists lynch ambitious vendors, commending their "valor" with patronizing praise and headlines that read "The little vendor that could!" before they send them on their way to rue the day that they tried to be something they were not.

Painfully aware of the push-cart vendor's predicament; unable to tell the media that he rescued "Madame Bardot" because his ex-wife is a bitch, Robin Fletcher settles on the following justification for his out-of-character heroism: "It's just my job."

36.

Fletcher focuses on the money.

"These pictures are gonna make you," he tells himself (which is a far better incentive than his earlier disingenuous mantra).

Even though he feels woozy, Robin Fletcher forces one last deep breath, flings open his car door, and plunges like a commando into the nearly empty street.

With his pulse throbbing in his temples, he hurriedly scampers over to the single row of withered bushes at the edge of the motel's parking lot. Quickly dropping to his knees, he wastes no time before falling to his belly.

Writhing like a snake, Fletcher maneuvers himself into a better view of "Madame Bardot's" motel room window.

He admits a few moments for her curtains to miraculously open, exposing the goings-on inside – Were he not plagued by his ex-wife's likely castigation, Robin Fletcher would give the pizza delivery man more time to reveal himself.

Tormented as he is though, Fletcher rises from his serpentine position and scurries over to the nearest corner of the motel; across which, he slides like a jumper on a building's ledge to just underneath "Madame Bardot's" window where he crouches.

Hunkered down; with his back pressed firmly to the wall, Fletcher cocks his head and strains to hear – But there is only silence from within.

Because Robin Fletcher's luck is shit, he grimaces.

Recognizing that he must inch himself up the motel's wall to peek inside (risking over-exposure and the ire of the pizza delivery man); knowing in his heart that he will never be called a man or a hero, Fletcher wants to reconsider everything, but he is unable – Licking at the soles of his feet, he feels the fire his ex-wife continually stokes (the fire wherein she burns him in effigy before their son at every opportunity); and he sees his cowardice like kerosene thrown on that pyre of derisory sentiment.

Even though there is the potential for a comparative windfall from the photographs; at this moment, fighting for air; managing painfully shallow, chest-burning breaths, Robin Fletcher only wants to be spared further ignominy in what was once his home.

37.

On the inside, "Madame Bardot's" motel window is caked in a decades old ochreous tobacco film deposited by smoking guests – At first inspection, it is impossible for Fletcher to see inside.

Pleased that he might just have to "phone this one in" (not wanting to personally interrupt if there is nothing concretely known to interrupt), Fletcher winces when he spies a faint, less-obstructed light emanating from an opening in the curtains. It is visible at a spot where children of guests likely pressed their faces, cleaning the carcinogenic resin off with their cheeks and fingers.

Because Robin Fletcher strongly believes that there is something inside "Madame Bardot's" motel room deserving of interruption, he quietly moans, "Shit" (even though the partition in the curtain affords him a coveted vantage point from which he might take pictures if there is no crime (other than against propriety) to report).

Straining his nerves, Fletcher creeps slowly towards his right, before inching up the motel wall.

Reaching the spot (a clean pane no larger than a child's round face through which the room's light escapes like a projector beam), Robin Fletcher sees "Madame Bardot".

Alive, uninjured, and naked; sitting cross-legged on the bed; smoking a cigarette; casually checking her cell phone text messages beside a half-empty pizza box filled with crusts and a revolver (Robin Fletcher remembers writing a blog about "Madame Bardot's" dislike of pizza crusts); overlooking the pizza delivery man sprawled face down with particles of his brain splattered against the motel wall, "Madame Bardot" cuts a striking figure.

Catching his breath for the first time in what seems an eternity, Fletcher sighs, "Thank God," before he snaps several photographs.

38.

Because "Madame Bardot" is safe; because he does not have to engage an imbalanced pizza delivery man, Robin Fletcher takes his time.

Because "Madame Bardot" is naked and he is armed with a camera, Fletcher does not feel threatened by her.

"She wouldn't come out here naked," he thinks.

Briefly, he considers phoning an ambulance for the pizza delivery man, but he decides against this. Though he is not a doctor, Robin Fletcher knows well enough that there is no treatment for a blown brain, so there is no reason to rush ("Besides, the cops will actually be grateful for this photographic evidence of mine.").

When he has taken as many pictures as he can; feeling very good about himself, Robin Fletcher stealthily withdraws back across the parking lot (this time around the bushes) to his car.

Lighting an herbal cigarette; phoning Information ("I must be the last man on Earth without an IPhone"), Fletcher connects with the motel office staff and alerts them of a commotion in "Madame Bardot's" room.

The young woman who answers asks to know his name – Because he knows the story of the push-cart vendor the way children know popular fables, Robin Fletcher chooses to remain anonymous: "You need to hurry, ma'am."

While patiently waiting for the authorities, Fletcher attempts to upload the digital photographs of "Madame Bardot" into his out-dated laptop.

He promises to invest in a newer model with the money earned.

While wondering how much his pictures will fetch in the bidding war ("I wonder how much [a popular gossip magazine] will pay?"), Robin Fletcher's too-old laptop overheats and crashes, taking with it every image of "Madame Bardot": The nude homicidal cutting a striking figure.

Having lost everything, Robin Fletcher loses his mind.

39.

People who have near-death experiences often report that their lives flashed before their eyes.

They are able to report because they did not actually die – They just nearly died.

People who really die do not generally have anything to say about the cusp at which life becomes death.

The living can tell us what happens when we almost die, but they cannot tell us what happens when we really do die (at least, not beyond a shadow of a doubt).

Because of that uncertainty, the living are free to speculate about what passes before the eyes of the man who actually dies; which could be any number of things.

Because the pizza delivery man actually died, there is no guarantee that his "life-lived" replayed. Neither is there is a solid reason to believe that he would regale us from the grave with stories of bright lights at the end of a tunnel.

In the split-second before "Madame Bardot's" bullet entered the back of his skull; bore through his brain; and then exploded through his face (embedding itself in the motel wall), the pizza delivery man might have seen something very different – He might have seen the life he would have lived had he been allowed to leave "Madame Bardot's" motel room - Maybe his "life-never-to-be-lived" flashed before the eyes of the pizza delivery man.

PART II.

1.

"You've been through a lot. Take the rest of the week off."

The pizza delivery man tells his boss that he is ready to work now: "I'm fine, really."

Impatient with his employee, the pizza delivery man's boss tells him that he is not doing him a courtesy: "Look, if it were up to me you'd be working tonight, but it's not. Company policy says you gotta take the rest of the week off."

An incoming call interrupts.

Abrasively, his boss reaches over the head of the pizza delivery man for the wall-mounted telephone, forcing him to duck and shuffle self-consciously out of the way.

While wondering if there is a corporate manual with a clause (some provision made for a thrill-seeking television personality's assault on a pizza delivery man that unnecessarily grants him the rest of the week off), his co-worker swings open the kitchen door; throws his red leather satchel on the flour-dusted counter-top; and counts his meager tips.

The two delivery men say nothing to each other.

2.

The pizza delivery man who is right now in the pizzeria's kitchen only exists in the soon-to-be-obliterated mind of the real pizza delivery man.

He exists in the blink of an eye: In that millisecond before the real pizza delivery man's brain erupts through his forehead thanks to "Madame Bardot".

At this moment, the pizza delivery man who challenges his employer for the right to work believes that he miraculously survived "Madame Bardot" and emerged entirely unscathed, marked only by the self-knowledge gained from the ordeal (that is, the understanding that he might have that "Something" within him or within his grasp).

This pizza delivery man does not know that he is only the real pizza delivery man's wishful thought

– He does not know that he is living the real pizza delivery man's "life-never-to-be-lived".

3.

After his boss hangs up the phone and relays the customer's order to his staff, the pizza delivery man uncharacteristically pushes the issue: "I need this work. I need to deliver pizzas."

Distracted by the demands of running a business; flipping through receipts for unaccounted profits and losses, his boss asks if the pizza delivery man is hurting for money: "Or something?"

Because he will never offer to help; because he does not actually care, the pizza delivery man's boss immediately regrets having asked.

Knowing that there could never be an offer of assistance on the proverbial table, the pizza delivery man simply answers, "Yeah, or something."

Clock-watching and feeling harassed, his boss aims to end the conversation: "What did I say? If it were up to me, you'd be working - I don't make the rules."

Told to come back next week, the pizza delivery man entreats, "Please, it's all I have."

Irritated (and more threatened by the wrath of corporate than moved by his employee's impassioned plea), the pizza delivery man's boss cruelly tells him to look around: "What do you see here? If this is all you got, then, pal, you got nothing."

Having been aroused at the hand of "Madame Bardot", the pizza delivery man knows that his boss is wrong.

4.

Ex nihilo is Latin. It means "out of nothing".

Most Christians, Muslims, and Jews believe that God made the world *ex nihilo* (that is, from nothing).

Before "Madame Bardot's" bullet; before his mind switched to auto-pilot and the real pizza delivery man began to watch his "life-never-to-be-lived", a layman's unformed notion of *ex nihilo* menacingly entered his thoughts.

Though the result of the pizza delivery man's fear of physical death (his fear of a return to the nothingness from whence he came), the notion of *ex nihilo* brought to his awareness another predicament: His survival.

Though the pizza delivery man honestly suspected that he might have that something (or be capable of making that something by which men are deemed important), he could not shake the suspicion that he might have nothing with which to work - And though unable to express the concept of "out of nothing" in Latin, the pizza delivery man knew it well enough to feel sick when he considered that the people who denigrated his job might be right.

Trembling in humility (not because he feared a return to nothingness, but rather the opposite: A stay of execution), the pizza delivery man nearly despaired beyond recovery when he considered the following: "I'm not fucking God. I can't make that something from nothing - What if I got nothing?"

Only "Madame Bardot's" Haitian-accented ring-tone snapped him out of his funk, reminding him of a university student with whom he once worked and a conversation they had had about pies.

5.

Upon hearing "Madame Bardot's" personalized ring-tone after she misquoted him ("You feel like a mule?"), the pizza delivery man remembered a baby-faced Haitian with whom he once delivered pizzas: A young pre-med student working his way through school.

From him, the pizza delivery man learned that Haitians make pies from dirt.

"Fuck off! Are you serious?"

Smiling, the baby-faced Haitian replied that he was very serious: "Though the dirt is special yellow dirt from Haiti's central plateau, it's still dirt – When wet, it's mud."

The pizza delivery man listened with rapt attention.

The baby-faced pre-med continued: "Poor Haitians mix the dirt with salt and vegetable shortening; form the mixture into pies; and then leave them to bake in the Caribbean sun.

"For the worse off, the pies are a staple.

"Because they treat more than hunger pangs (counter-acting excessive and debilitating stomach acidity and supplementing calcium), the pies are also medicinal.

"Some of them even like the salty, butter-like taste" – Removing his corporate-issued baseball cap, the baby-faced university student really wanted it to be known that he was not a poor Haitian: "At least, some of them must."

6.

Sometimes necessity is more than the mother of invention – Sometimes she is the mother of right perception.

Originally, when the pizza delivery man heard that story about the Haitian mud pies, he thought, "Miraculous!" – However, when he found himself at the business-end of "Madame Bardot's" revolver; when he remembered that story about the Haitian mud pies, he thought, "Amazing, but do-able."

The pizza delivery man downgraded the Haitians' mud pies from "Miraculous!" to "Amazing, but do-able" because he finally came to see them for what they were.

From the start, the pizza delivery man had thought the Haitians reached down into their soil and, from nothing, miraculously made food: The mud pie.

For many years, he had likened the starving Haitians with God Who reached down into the soil to make a man.

However, when he was on his knees before "Madame Bardot"; when his heart was paralyzed with self-doubt, questioning how he could make something from nothing (like God or a starving Haitian), something clicked in the pizza delivery man's mind.

Like a cornered animal discovering an extra ounce of fight; listening to "Madame Bardot's" ring-tone; remembering the baby-faced medical student, the pizza delivery man found his doors of perception swung wide open, revealing to him this simple, yet over-looked fact: Dirt is not nothing – It is just a very modest something.

With new awareness; inspired by the Haitians, rather than humbled by them; inspired by God, the pizza delivery man resolved then-and-there to reach down into his own very modest something and make himself a whole man ("As soon as I get out of this.").

7.

When the pizza delivery man in this "life-never-to-be-lived" told his boss, "It's all I have," he meant "Delivering pizzas is my very modest something. Unlike God, I cannot make anything from nothing, and I most certainly cannot make that something from nothing. Even though delivering pizzas is next to dirt, it is still a thing in which or from which I might find myself a whole man."

Even if he had not been spared all of that subtext, the pizza delivery man's boss would still have responded, "Get the fuck out of here before I fire your queer ass!" and he would still have meant just this.

8.

Several months before the "Madame Bardot" incident, the pizza delivery man met Robin Fletcher.

Fletcher had been tailing a famous politician's improvident son all day, and (having parked outside the young man's condominium for the night) he had begun to drink – He had begun to drink because he was only a few weeks into his new life as a bachelor and he was having difficulty convincing himself that he could not be happier.

Needing to make it through the night without passing out, Fletcher decided that he should not drink so heavily on an empty stomach.

Having been held up by traffic; when the pizza delivery man located the intersection and car to which the pizzeria had directed him, he found a shit-faced Robin Fletcher at the wheel acting guardedly in the dark: "Hey man, did you order a pizza?"

To which, Robin Fletcher snarled through the open driver-side window, "Can't you see I'm jacking off? Why don't you take a fucking picture?"

Having seen worse on the job, the pizza delivery man responded that he did not have a camera, and then produced a deep-dish pizza pie from his red leather satchel: "Alright, that'll be-"

But before he could quote the price, Fletcher thrust his camera at the pizza delivery man's face, narrowly missing his nose: "No excuses – Take a fucking picture."

Wondering who would want to see a photograph of a drunkard masturbating in his car, the pizza delivery man asked Fletcher if he was someone important: "Who happens to drive a beat-up piece of shit?"

Upon having the question put to him so pointedly, Robin Fletcher broke down.

That night, bawling in his drunkenness; knowing that no one would want a photo of him pleasuring himself, Robin Fletcher confessed to the pizza delivery man something that he had managed to keep hidden even from his sober self: "I'm a nobody – Just a *paparazzo*: A parasite."

Painfully acquainted with the misery of unimportance, the pizza delivery man walked to the passenger side of Fletcher's car; opened the door; slid in beside the sad stranger; and volunteered his deep-dish pizza pie: "Free of charge."

Touched by the unexpected charity, Fletcher insisted that the two share: "Especially considering," he weakly joked, staring down at his circumcised penis, "I don't seem to have a tip."

Though Robin Fletcher woke the next morning with a hangover and absolutely no recollection of the charitable pizza delivery man, the pizza delivery man would carry with him (till the day he died) the memory of a man with whom he shared a slice of pizza and something like brotherly commiseration, if not love.

9.

Rather than be fired, the pizza delivery man in this "life-never-to-be-lived" heads home.

Driving back to his apartment, he notices a beat-up piece of shit in his rear-view mirror.

Curious as to why the *paparazzo* (for whom he never got a name) would be interested in him, the pizza delivery man signals his intention before merging onto the hard shoulder and parking.

When Robin Fletcher comes to a complete stop, the pizza delivery man exits his car and walks back towards him.

Reaching Fletcher's car, the pizza delivery man is saddened to find his old acquaintance, like an Alzheimer's patient, nervously locking his doors – And, yet, stupidly leaving his window down.

Anticipating an altercation (still snapping away furiously with his camera), Fletcher tells the pizza delivery man that he only wants to talk: "With the man who survived [Madame Bardot]."

Shielding his eyes from the *paparazzo's* point-blank flash photography, the pizza delivery man informs Fletcher that he has already given his statement to the police: "It was self-defense. I only fought back."

A crowded bus, filled with teenagers, speeds past – "Cock-suckers!" they shout.

Spitting out a wad of nicotine gum, Robin Fletcher scowls before fighting back to as near an impassive face as he can muster: "Yeah, that's what

you told the cops, but everyone knows differently –
What really happened in that motel room?"

Exercising his right to remain silent, the pizza
delivery man turns to walk back towards his car when
Fletcher suddenly grabs him by the wrist: "You're a
fraud, pizza boy. No one believes you."

Prying himself from the *paparazzo's* grip, the
pizza delivery man reminds Fletcher that the police
must: "Otherwise, I'd be in jail right now, dip-shit."

Because the pizza delivery man
misunderstands him, Fletcher laughs: "The revolver
belonged to [Madame Bardot]. They even found the
receipt in her purse – No one thinks you murdered
her."

A half-empty soda can thrown from a passing
car pelts the pizza delivery man on his right shoulder
– Curling backwards for the stinging pain, he
demands to know: "Just what the hell are you getting
at, *paparazzo*?"

Still left with a foul taste in his mouth from the
nicotine-infused chewing gum, Fletcher spits, "I'm a
fucking photojournalist, cunt-rag!" before he tells the

pizza delivery man at what he is getting: "It was an accident, wasn't it?"

Truly pissed-off by this man with whom he once shared a deep-dish pizza pie, the pizza delivery man snaps, "I fought back!" before he stomps back towards his own car.

Even with the sound of highway traffic, the pizza delivery man still hears the *paparazzo* shouting, "In your fucking dreams, pizza boy! - Men like you don't fight back!"

10.

Goethe, the German *homo universalis*, said that "Talent is best nurtured in solitude."

In that respect, one can anthropomorphize Being-In-Solitude – She is like a maternal woman caring for her charge.

However, if a man does not have a talent, then Being-In-Solitude is like a childless woman with maternal instincts.

Because Being-In-Solitude exists in the absence of another human being, perhaps it is more fitting to liken her to an animal – Perhaps the pizza delivery man (alone now in his dark, squalid studio apartment) is in the embrace of a childless and hormonal female gorilla.

11.

However strange, the constructed analogy between a childless gorilla and Being-In-Solitude is surprisingly appropriate.

Sometimes a gorilla that delivers a still-born will carry the dead baby; bring it to her teat; and try to suckle it. When the gorilla accepts that her baby is dead (or when the baby decomposes into nothing), she abandons it.

Likewise, when Being-In-Solitude cannot deny that a man's talent is still-born, she, too, abandons it.

However, though both gorilla and Being-In-Solitude discard their dead babies, neither can put aside their need to nurture.

Just as a distraught female gorilla adopts orphaned baby gorillas (sometimes adopting and caring for animals from other species, like kittens); so, too, does Being-In-Solitude seek something else in a talentless man for which to help care.

At this moment; sitting on his bean bag chair, the pizza delivery man feels like he is being groomed by a desperate gorilla searching his person for a sign of life.

12.

The gorilla metaphor illustrates three important aspects of the pizza delivery man's isolation: 1) It shows that, even when alone, the pizza delivery man feels like he is in the company of a disappointed female; 2) It correlates the habitats of talentless men with the jungles and zoos wherein gorillas live; and 3) It draws attention to Being-In-Solitude's gorilla-like protective distance from human beings, as if all men and women were poachers preying on pizza delivery men.

Of course, because understanding something in terms of another thing is an incomplete understanding, the gorilla analogy is not enough – Another metaphor is needed to explain that characteristic of Being-In-Solitude that is not like a desperately seeking mother.

13.

When prison wardens want to punish an inmate, they often put him in solitary confinement – That is, they hand him over to Being-In-Solitude.

Goethe was not thinking of solitary confinement when he was thinking of solitude; he was thinking about a craftsman's secluded space, free from diversions, filled with the instruments of his trade.

However, because the pizza delivery man is not a talented craftsman; because he could not afford the tools or the time off from work even if he were, his Being-In-Solitude is not an innocuous isolated space – Free from diversions within, as much as it is free from diversions without, the pizza delivery man's small, studio apartment is also a terrifying place of sensory deprivation: A room for psychological torture.

Because psychological torture always has physical ramifications, Being-In-Solitude exacts a hellish toll on the pizza delivery man for his disobedience: Being unimportant when he should be otherwise.

Arguably, Lockdown (as solitary confinement is known) is Hell on Earth.

Because of that, the prisoner in solitary confinement (or the pizza delivery man with a week's vacation) must feel that his overseer is the Devil himself.

14.

In the embrace of a desperately seeking gorilla who does not know her own strength; wanting so badly to give her something in him to love (something to stop her anxious hands from crushing his throat and making it hard to breathe); feeling like he has been hauled to the jungle's canopy, from which he dangerously hangs; tormented by the Devil for the sin of being unimportant; alone in his dismal, cell-like apartment with idle hands (with these the Devil's very playground); it should not surprise anyone that the pizza delivery man (so like Goethe's Faust) reaches out to sell his soul: "I'd like to order a pizza, please."

15.

A pizza delivery man is like a messenger.

Messengers are historically relevant. In the histories of families, communities, nations, and other organizations, messengers play a significant part – They move history along.

Even when they are killed, the deaths of messengers (which prevent messages from being delivered or send different messages all together) impact history.

And yet, unless the messenger is a Messenger of God (or the rare and athletic Pheidippides), he is largely unappreciated – A man can be historically relevant and still be dismissed.

When civilized men spare the messenger, they do so for the reason that uncivilized men once killed him: His unimportance (which is not historical unimportance; it is just the messenger's personal worthlessness - Consider the pawn in a game of chess or a foot-soldier in an army).

Arguably, the messenger is worthless because he is easily replaced; he is not unique.

When a messenger refuses to deliver a message (that is, if he refuses to be historically relevant), then another man (a *scab*) simply takes his place.

When understood in that light (as the cause of a worthless man's worthlessness), the *scab* is the unimportant man's deepest wound.

16.

"You son of a bitch!"

Cowering beside the empty industrial site's waste skip, the pizza delivery man's co-worker shields his head from another blow: "[Pizza delivery man], don't…"

Because he struggles not to sympathize with his co-worker's powerlessness, the pizza delivery man staggers backwards; lowers his bloodied baseball bat, converting it into a makeshift cane to support his physically and emotionally exhausted person; and tries to remember all that is at stake.

While his very probably concussed co-worker pathetically blubbers on hands and knees, the pizza delivery man reminds himself why he called the pizzeria from a pay-phone several blocks from his apartment; placed an order under an assumed name;

and gave the new guy the address to this construction site, which he knew would be deserted tonight: "That's right - I'm getting my fucking job back."

With renewed purpose (after all, his job is the only thing by which he might make himself a whole man; by which he might make himself important), the pizza delivery man marches back to his addled co-worker; squares off with his target, assuming a strong position with knees bent; firmly grips the bat with both hands; and swings it above his head in preparation for the fatal chopping motion: That crushing blow that will kill the *scab*.

Only the whimpering of a man that sounds so much like his own ("[Pizza delivery man], why?") stops him.

Raised by television and films, the suddenly dazed pizza delivery man feels like one of those fortunate villains who has been given the chance to explain himself – He feels like he has been given the opportunity to be understood, which is so important for a man's conscience.

17.

In French, the expression is *"Tout comprendre c'est tout pardonner"*.

For the Germans, it is *"Was wir verstehen, das können wir nicht tadeln"*.

In English, we form the proverb like this: "To understand everything is to forgive".

For the gob-smacked pizza delivery man who has been asked, "Why?" by his co-worker, there is now a chance to make himself understood by his victim and subsequently to be forgiven.

In the pizza delivery man's mind, there is the opportunity (however small) to bring his co-worker around to seeing things his way, perhaps even teasing a consensus from the whimpering *scab*.

"If I play my cards right," thinks the pizza delivery man, "I might just get this son of a bitch to admit that he deserves to be murdered."

Having paused for a moment to gather his thoughts; having taken the time necessary to unlock those secret words that will bring his victim into agreement with him and thereby cleanse himself of the sin, the pizza delivery man finally answers his co-worker: "Because you took my fucking job, and everyone knows that ain't right, motherfucker!"

18.

"I didn't take your fucking job!"

The pizza delivery man asks his co-worker to repeat himself because his words were lost in the blood, spit and bile pouring from his mouth: "[Pizza delivery man], I didn't take your fucking job – I swear!"

Disgusted by what he thinks is a bold-faced lie, the pizza delivery man demands that his co-worker not take him for a fool: "Motherfucker, you're working my shift!"

"Shift!" exclaims his co-worker. "That's all! – You're coming back next week; they said you're coming back next week – Christ, you're coming back next week, right?"

Menacingly turning the baseball bat in his hands; twisting a sinew-like sound from its cloth grip, the pizza delivery man answers, "Yeah, I'm coming back next week."

Confused, his co-worker shudders and then vomits again before begging to know why the pizza delivery man cannot wait – He begs because he cannot see the dissatisfied gorilla breathing on the pizza delivery man's neck; and because he cannot hear the Devil whispering in his bat-wielding co-worker's ear, "You've already waited a lifetime, maybe your *entire* lifetime. Kill the *scab* – You can't be talented, but you can be rare!"

19.

What is the pizza delivery man's "life-never-to-be-lived"?

Is it a dream? A simple figment of his imagination before "Madame Bardot's" bullet punctures his cranium?

If it is a dream, what kind of dream is it? – Is it one over which he has absolute, partial, or no dominion? - How much of it is the product of his conscious mind? How much is the product of his unconscious?

Is it like a dream in the deepest sleep? Or is it a day-dream?

Or is the pizza delivery man's "life-never-to-be-lived" an extradimensional reality?

Is it a realm apart, set aside for him to realize the manhood that eluded him in the real world?

20.

Looking down at his co-worker's yellow river of sick pooling at his feet (as yellow as his number 7), the pizza delivery man finds in the swirling bile suds, like Proustian madeleines, a remembrance of things past.

21.

Before he delivered pizzas, the pizza delivery man's co-worker answered phones at a call center.

He had a work station with a computer, a telephone headset, and photographs of his then pregnant wife.

Although none of his employees personally met customers, the call center's supervisor still insisted that everyone dress professionally: "The customers can hear a straight tie."

Because the supervisor required all of his employees to dress uncomfortably most of the time and made them dress comfortably some of the time ("Casual Dress Fridays"), almost all of them loved him – All of them except the pizza delivery man's co-worker.

The pizza delivery man's co-worker did not loathe his supervisor because he had a natural resistance to the Stockholm Syndrome, but rather because dressing uncomfortably in pressed pants and starched collars gave him the opportunity to role play.

Earning too little for an expectant father; working from an impersonal script; without any real benefits; suffering customers' complaints day-in and day-out; scrutinized by the unforgiving supervisor, the pizza delivery man's co-worker only had uncomfortable clothes to help him feel better in his own skin – Dressing like a businessman (even though he was not a businessman) gave him a degree of cache at McDonald's.

On Casual Dress Fridays; standing in line for that single McChicken sandwich he could afford; dressed in worn jeans and sneakers, the pizza delivery man's co-worker felt like shit, and it was all his boss' fault.

Weekends after Casual Dress Fridays were rough, spent trying to look on the bright side.

"Alright," the pizza delivery man's co-worker often said to himself, "because of the company's skills-based routing system, in-bound calls are sent to specialist agents – And I am one of those specialists. I am special. So what if I'm not a third-tier customer support provider (an engineer or developer)? I'm still relatively well-positioned – "Newbies" look to me for veteran counsel."

Sometimes the pizza delivery man's co-worker made himself feel better.

The day that his job was out-sourced to India, he even thought about finding another call center position – That is, until his great with child wife answered the door, and her water broke on his tattered converse shoes; it was a Friday.

Seeing that he needed a job with more security, the pizza delivery man's co-worker decided to deliver pizzas: "Delivering pizzas is the only job that you can't pay an Untouchable in India to do." 22.

"Delivering pizzas is the only job that you can't pay an Untouchable in India to do."

His co-worker knows that he is being quoted, but he does not know why, nor does he care: "Can I have another ice pack?"

In his small apartment, the pizza delivery man does not have to move far to reach the mini-fridge. He removes the ice tray and drops the last cubes into another dish towel.

Handing his co-worker the homemade ice pack, the pizza delivery man asks him if he is doing any better: "Still seeing double?"

Squinting for the dim light given-off by the single bulb hanging overhead that illuminates only half of the apartment; still overcome by a wave of nausea when he moves his neck, the pizza delivery man's co-worker replies from between his knees, "Unless I have two pairs of feet, I'm seeing double" adding that he probably should not be allowed to fall asleep tonight.

Ignoring him, the pizza delivery man crouches on the floor beside his hotplate at a stack of magazines.

Sifting through the pile, he asks, "[My co-worker], have I ever told you that I'm a synesthete?"

Even though he does not believe in telepathy, the pizza delivery man's co-worker decides it is best to humor the man who only an hour ago was beating him with a Louisville slugger: "That's great – So what am I thinking of now?"

Chalking-up his co-worker's question to him having a rattled brain, the pizza delivery man explains that a synesthete is not a telepath: "I don't read minds, asshole – I see colors when I see numbers and letters, when I see graphemes."

"Ah," sighs his co-worker, somewhat relieved not to be dealing with a man who believes he has psychic powers. "And you're telling me this because?"

"Because," says the pizza delivery man, "Grapheme-color synesthesia saved your life."
23.

Having found the issue of **Psychological Science** for which he was looking, the pizza delivery man opens it to a page he has dog-eared, and then passes it to his co-worker: "Here, read this and get your mind blown."

Astounded by the insensitivity, his co-worker reminds him that he is still seeing double: "So how the fuck am I supposed to read anything?"

The pizza delivery man apologizes – He asks if he should read the article aloud.

Exhausted by the whole business, the pizza delivery man's co-worker begrudgingly answers, "Sure, man - Whatever."

Flipping through the article's many pages with their small, dense print (the few words he ever read in college and only because the subject matter applied directly to him), the pizza delivery man has a change of heart: "Look, why don't I just give you the gist?"

Unresisted, the pizza delivery man puts the findings of the University of Waterloo into his own words: "Synesthetes don't all see the same color when they see the same character – When one sees green another sees blue. Still, most of us do share a way of seeing; which we share with non-synesthetes.

"Basically, this doctor, Dr. David Smilek, did an experiment. He made a group of non-synesthetes (people who don't see colors when they see letters and numbers); he made them give a color to certain graphemes, and then he had them arrange the graphemes in order of brightness."

The pizza delivery man's co-worker rubs his sore head, not knowing what to make of this nonsense: "And this shit saved my life?"

"Dr. Smilek," continues the pizza delivery man, "discovered that non-synesthetes, just like synesthetes, find the more *commonly* used letters and numbers to be brighter."

The pizza delivery man moves to be nearer his co-worker: "When I stood in your pool of yellow bile (the color of my number 7); when it reminded me of your wife's water breaking on your shoes; when I remembered your remark about the Untouchables in India, I saw something in you."

"And what was that?" asks his co-worker, somewhat intrigued now by the prospect of having something inside himself.

"I saw a man like me – Just a common fuck."
24.

"You didn't kill me because you saw a common fuck inside me?"

Returning to his bean bag chair, the pizza delivery man tells his co-worker that he did not kill him ("even though there is this hellish temptation to be rare") because he cannot do away with all the pizza delivery men on earth, "But mostly because without you, even though I'd be more rare, I'd also be less common."

The pizza delivery man's co-worker does not understand: "That doesn't make any fucking sense – No man wants to be more common."

Thumping the article on Dr. Smilek's Grapheme-color synesthesia research with his knuckles, the pizza delivery man grins: "That's because, [My co-worker], men like you don't appreciate that the common can be fucking brilliant!"

PART III.

1.

According to Ilinca Zarifopol-Johnston in her
book *Searching for Cioran (2008)*; when Romanian-
born author, E.M. Cioran, wrote his fascist work,
Romania's Transfiguration in 1937, he wanted his
countrymen "to draw their strength from the 'lucidity
of beginnings,' that is, the consciousness of absence of
noble origins".

For Zarifopol-Johnston, "[Cioran's] emphasis
is on a profound sense of emptiness before the
struggle rather than (as might seem normal) on a
sense of achieved fullness to follow. If they
[Romanians] are to be creators, they must be
'divinely' aware of being creators ex nihilo".

Provided Zarifopol-Johnston has faithfully
relayed his sentiment, it can be said that Cioran
pulled a Cioran (meaning, he exaggerated); he
hyperbolically associated the nothingness from which
God created the universe with the earlier Romanians'
supposed lack of something of which to be proud –

Arguably, only Cioran held such a negative opinion of his antecedents.

Though patently an exaggeration, the lack of something of which to be proud is a nothing from which the "profound sense of emptiness" (or "the consciousness of absence of noble origins") can emerge with a materiality as real to a man as a lead pipe swung directly into his gut – It is likely that with this metal embedded in their alimentary canals Cioran expected marginalized people (like his fellow Romanians; like pizza delivery men) to be hardened and emboldened to act, even atrociously.

2.

When the pizza delivery man's boss dies, his muscles that had been holding in the urine and feces relax, soiling himself and the backseat of the car: "Motherfucker, [Pizza delivery man]! He shit in my car – The fucker shit in my car!"

Intently focusing on the rain-slicked road ahead, the pizza delivery man tells his co-worker to quit his bitching: "What the fuck did you expect?! – Crack a window."

Cursing the warm puddle of urine sloshing against his thigh; disentangling his hands from the guitar string garrote with which he strangled their boss, the pizza delivery man's co-worker fumbles in the dark for the power window switch: "Damnit! [Pizza delivery man], my wife was driving the car last – You're gonna have to open the window from up there."

Impatient; nearly overcome by the stench, the pizza delivery man's co-worker snaps, "For fucks sake! It's on the panel just below the radio controls."

Leaning across the steering wheel, the pizza delivery man first wipes down the fogged-up windshield before reaching for the power windows' main switch.

Rolling down all four windows, he digs into his co-worker: "Asshole, I told you to wait!" and then hammers into the dashboard with his fist: "Shit! Shit!"

"Take it easy, [Pizza delivery man]! You saw the way he was kicking and banging around. If he'd kept that shit up we'd have crashed miles back – I saved our fucking lives!"

Glaring into the rear-view mirror, the pizza delivery man says nothing – He just rolls the windows back up.

His co-worker responds: "You're a real bitch, you know that?"

3.

When the pizza delivery man's "divinely aware" co-worker said that he saved their lives, he was arguing on the grounds that self-defense is an acceptable reason for killing a man.

When his boss was kicking furiously against the back of the pizza delivery man's seat and headrest, he was resisting without compunction because self-defense is an acceptably rational motive for trying to kill two kidnappers who, in the course of their careless conversation, let it slip that they intend to murder the kidnapped in an isolated wood ("[Pizza delivery man], I figured we could use this guitar string instead of the plastic bag that's got holes in it.").

Even the pizza delivery man, when he killed "Madame Bardot", did so because he expected justification in the eyes of the law for the simple reason that self-defense excuses homicide – He knew that old chestnut ("I had no choice – It was her or me.") would remove culpability.

Because of that, do not misconstrue the pizza delivery man's turmoil as a wholesale disagreement with the rightness of defending oneself – The pizza delivery man repeatedly punched the dashboard only because he knew that his co-worker's lethal countermeasure could not hope to avail itself of this convincing argument.

"Shit! Shit!" was the pizza delivery man giving voice to his appreciation that (however much it would have inconvenienced them) he and his co-worker could have abandoned Plan B, thereby defusing their boss' aggressive behavior – He did not have to die.

Right now, the pizza delivery man is extremely disturbed because he knows that the strangulation of their boss was only weakly self-defense – He is agitated because he knows that it was really self-interest.

4.

"Shit! Shit!" was also a nervous vocal tic, triggered by the pizza delivery man's recognition that his mental state (his *mens rea*) leading up to his boss' death would likely be adjudged by a jury of his peers to possess malice aforethought even though that was not completely true.

Even though the pizza delivery man had conspired to murder their boss in defense of their interests; even though Plan B was his idea; up until the death of his employer (signaled by the vacuation of the man's bowels), he still harbored hope for a miracle.

Remember: The pizza delivery man struggled against his compassion when he tried to murder his co-worker for the sake of rarity and its resultant importance.

"Shit! Shit!" was the pizza delivery man (as if emerging from a fog) clearly reckoning that the long drive to an isolated wood would never be seen by another as a stalling tactic (which it was): A sign of good faith: An opportunity for God to stop them – For the pizza delivery man, the long drive was not fully Plan B, but rather Plan A with an eye towards Plan B ("But still part of a civil fucking negotiation!").

Right up to the end, the pizza delivery man had hoped that God would intervene (much as He did for Abraham at the binding of Isaac); that He would spare the life of their boss, while still bestowing significance upon him; and that He would free him from the onerous business of defending an interest – Which, for an unimportant man, is an impossible task.

The pizza delivery man vented his frustration on the car's dashboard because he knew that men like him are only permitted to fight for survival.

5.

When the pizza delivery man beat the dashboard, his exact feeling (though he seemed outraged to his co-worker) was not fury; it was despondency – However disappointed the pizza delivery man was to have the condemnation of the law hanging above his head, this condemnation (which only threatened him with imprisonment and public censure: Both mere details for an unimportant man living in squalor) meant comparatively little – What distressed the pizza delivery man more was the hash-smoking Congolese "freedom fighter" he now felt was sitting beside him in the passenger seat.

6.

At the last gasp of his dying boss, the pizza delivery man heard what sounded like rustling foliage, a grown man shouting, and the faint cheerless singing of young recruits drilling – The childless gorilla that had been wringing his neck for her sadness heard as much because she released the pizza delivery man, flung open the passenger side door, and threw herself into the night (rolling like a rough-landing parachutist, seeking shelter in the nearest undergrowth).

When the pizza delivery man turned to check his side-view mirror to see if she had survived the jump from the moving automobile, he came face-to-face with the battle-scarred Congolese "freedom fighter" who had taken her place: The man who drove a 500 pound gorilla to seek cover for fear.

Taking a deep drag on his hash and cannabis bud joint, the "freedom fighter" outstretched his spindly arm, wrapped it around the pizza delivery man and announced, like a perverse godfather, how happy he was to be present: "At my new god-child's baptism in blood.

"You're not a fucking *Ilunga* anymore, [Pizza delivery man]! You're one of us – And no one is going to fuck with you now."

7.

In the South-East of the Democratic Republic of the Congo; in the Kasaï Occidental and Kasaï Oriental provinces, nearly 10 million people speak the Tshiluba language.

When the Congolese "freedom fighter" said that the pizza delivery man was no longer an *Ilunga*, he was speaking Tshiluba.

According to a thousand or so linguists (professors and the like), the word *Ilunga* is the most challenging word to translate – They define it as "a

person who is ready to forgive any abuse for the first
time, to tolerate it a second time, but never a third
time".

Arguably, linguists struggle to translate the
word *Ilunga* only because they cannot imagine a
western man who would forgive *any* abuse the first
time, let alone a second time – They struggle because
they cannot imagine a western man who would take
anything up the ass, and then pardon the offender.

Really, *Ilunga* is not a difficult word to
translate: "It's a pizza delivery man (maybe with a
lower threshold for pain)."

8.

Because the pizza delivery man knows that he
has not essentially changed; because he knows that
only his circumstances have changed as a result of his
boss' murder, he suspects that he cannot have
stopped being whatever the fuck an *Ilunga* is – He
suspects that he has only been impressed into a
Congolese army of child soldiers: Terrified boys
violently resisting the creatures that go bump in the
night

Speeding through the steady downpour (thick like a velour theater curtain closed in the guillotine style), the pizza delivery man's godfather drills into his ear: "You are a killing machine, and you are going to march, motherfucker! Because if you fall behind, this jungle," – The Congolese "freedom fighter" sweeps his sickly thin arm out across the breadth of the visible horizon – "This jungle, filled with childless gorillas, will swoop down and smother you in disappointment!

"*Tu me comprends?*"

The pizza delivery man does not understand French – He only understands the consequences of not marching forward.

9.

Unimportant men must choose between guaranteed suffocation at the hands of a despairing and hormonal gorilla or an uncertain rebellion led by a "freedom fighter" burning psychoactive drugs in poorly ventilated spaces.

Having killed their boss, the pizza delivery man and his co-worker decisively joined the latter camp.

When the pizza delivery man rolled up the car windows, it was not so much an expression of disapproval directed at his co-worker as it was him starting his training.

For the newly conscripted pizza delivery man, the entire world (visible through his windshield) had become a steamy, sealed car at night on a rain slicked road filled with death, piss and shit – And because good soldiers prepare for eventualities, he reasoned that they most assuredly prepared for certainties, as well: "Breathe deep, [My co-worker] – It's probably not gonna get any better than this."

10.

Clumsily, the pizza delivery man slices into the forehead of his boss: "Fuck me!"

His co-worker tells him not to get so upset ("I don't think he felt it.") before he resumes shoveling the water-logged mud onto their soon-to-be-interred former employer: "Come on, let's get this over with – We still need to find a 24-hour carwash."

Over his co-worker's shoulder, the pizza delivery man believes that he sees the Congolese "freedom fighter" sitting with his back against a tree, like the overseer of a small alluvial diamond mine in a conflict zone.

With rivulets of rain and perspiration trickling down his face (and the odd tear for his conscription), the pizza delivery man scoops another pile of mud onto the man who once tried to convince him that he had nothing.

Landing with a thud on his dead boss' expressionless face, the drenched clay, like an oil slick, reflects up to the pizza delivery man a perfect silhouette of himself back-lit by the car's headlights.

Knee-deep in this muddy miasma of death, the pizza delivery man is surprised to discover in his reflection a beatific halo surrounding his body.

Pissed-off to be burying their boss by himself; worrying about the headlights which drain the car battery; feeling increasingly put-upon by the expectation to return a spotless vehicle to his wife, the pizza delivery man's co-worker shouts, "Man, I'm not doing this alone – Come on, put your fucking back into it!" – But his words fall on deaf ears.

The pizza delivery man is transfixed – Entranced by his reflection, he stands in the rain (in the grave of his dead boss) like a zombie under the influence of some dissociative drug (as if his mind were caught up in the downpour's muddied runoff).

Though the rainwater finally washes away his aura-encircled reflection, the pizza delivery man remains under its spell – Ignoring the exhortations of his co-worker to continue burying their boss ("Before the damn things overflows!"), the pizza delivery man drops his shovel; reaches down into a patch of dark mud (a blood red copper when dry); and grabs a handful of wet earth at which he frantically claws until he reveals what (to him) appears to be a diamond.

Turning his discovery over in his hand, the pizza delivery man holds it up for his bewildered co-worker to inspect: "Look at this fucking beauty!"

Immediately, he regrets having been so loud –
Out of the corner of his eye, he believes he catches the
shape of the Congolese "freedom fighter" bounding
towards him, intent on stealing the find.

Panicked, the pizza delivery man quickly
clenches his fist, puncturing his soft palm with such
force that blood squirts from out of his knuckles like
he had squeezed a tomato.

"What the fuck, [Pizza delivery man]!"

His co-worker's shock coupled with the
searing pain in his bloodied hand breaks the spell
under which the pizza delivery man labored.

Looking up, he sees that the Congolese
"freedom fighter" has not left his spot beside the tree
– He also sees his co-worker staring at him with an
expression of extreme unease.

His co-worker demands to know what the
pizza delivery man's fucking problem is: "Have you
lost your fucking mind?"

Defensively, the pizza delivery man insists
that he has not lost his fucking mind: "I just thought-"

Slowly, he rolls open his bloodied fist with his other hand - Both men observe the depth of the gash made by the broken glass.

"Jesus."

Slightly nauseous, the pizza delivery man tries to explain, while picking shards: "I just thought I'd found something else"

Grumbling that men like them are not that lucky, the pizza delivery man's co-worker hoists his shovel into the air and brings it down into the open palm of their insentient former boss, severing four fingers.

He collects the disembodied digits into the plastic bag: "[Pizza delivery man], we're running out of time – This was your idea, remember?"

Examining his blackened hand and the particulates of glass he mistook for a single diamond, the pizza delivery man apologizes: "Hand me my shovel, will you?"

11.

In the spring of 1891, Pope Leo XIII issued his famous encyclical **Rerum Novarum**, which addressed the miserable conditions of the *fin-de-siècle* working classes.

Although **Rerum Novarum** (which is Latin for "Of New Things") defended the right of working men to unionize, it expressly forbade violence as a means to eradicate "the utter poverty of the masses":

> "Of these duties, the following bind the proletarian and the worker: fully and faithfully to perform the work which has been freely and equitably agreed upon; never to injure the property, nor to outrage the person, of an employer; never to resort to violence in defending their own cause, nor to engage in riot or disorder; and to have nothing to do with men of evil principles, who work upon the people with artful promises of great results, and excite foolish hopes which usually end in useless regrets and grievous loss."

Having been raised a Catholic; having resorted to violence in defending his cause; having certainly outraged the person of his employer; dropping the last shovelfuls of mud onto his boss' unmarked final resting place, the pizza delivery man feels like he has formed an all together different union than intended.

In his ear, the Devil asks, "Now what?"

To which, the pizza delivery man answers, "Now we phone [The new guy]."

Because he did not ask a question, the pizza delivery man's co-worker has to assume he has been given an order – He pats down the grave one last time and walks back to the car.

12.

Hours before they kidnapped and murdered their boss, the pizza delivery man and his co-worker had sought out the new guy: A recent high school graduate who had started delivering pizza pies because his mother did not approve of his wish to be a celebrity blogger.

They had cornered the young man outside the rear entrance of the pizzeria right before his night-shift began, swarming to him like moths to a brilliant flame.

"[New guy], you got a minute?"

Because it was still early and the pizzeria's phone had not started ringing, the new guy answered that he had a minute, and then added that he was glad to hear that the pizza delivery man was not killed: "Even though [Madame Bardot] was my favorite!"

The pizza delivery man imagined the new guy's Facebook presence – In his mind's eye, he saw a page filled with the new guy's likes and dislikes: His self-indentifying consumerism: His autobiography constructed from other people's biographies.

For a moment, looking into the new guy's somewhat sorrowful eyes, the pizza delivery man thought, "He must have died a little when I did not die at all."

When, like a eulogist gathering notes (or a sycophantic celebrity blogger), the new guy asked about "Madame Bardot's" appearance ("Was she as beautiful in person?"), the pizza delivery man could not answer – Social networking had made him feel like a serial murderer; he wondered how many condolences had been tweeted through cyber-space by people whom he had likewise killed a little simply by staying alive.

Nervously, the pizza delivery man switched gears and cut straight to the chase: "We're starting a union – Are you in?"

13.

At first, the new guy said, "No."

Apart from his belief that the pizza delivery man and his co-worker were not an authority deserving of a "Yes", the new guy said "No" because he was risk averse – He knew that delivering pizzas required little skill; as a result, it would be easy for their boss to fire them all and hire replacements – Which is not to say that the new guy did not want to be fired eventually.

Even though he did not wish to be (even though he did not envision himself as he was so young) delivering pizza pies for much longer; even though the prospect of a *scab* on the horizon loomed far less menacingly for him than for the older pizza delivery man and his co-worker, the new guy resisted joining the union simply because he did not want to face the ire of his mother: "She'd kill me if I got fired, [Pizza delivery man]."

Infuriated by his admission, the pizza delivery man's co-worker grabbed the new guy by the collar and threatened: "I'm gonna fucking kill you, you little queer, if you fuck this up for me!"

Alarmed by the eruption of a man known to have once answered phones at a call center, the new guy turned to the pizza delivery man as if to beg "You gotta help me out here" – But the pizza delivery man, disinterested in the good cop/bad cop routine, just sucker punched the restrained new guy in the kidney: "Fuck your mom – Everyone else has!" before he instructed his co-worker to drag the crumpled teenager across the road in the direction of an abandoned and overgrown lot: "Where the street-lights are all burnt out."

The new guy fell hard at the edge of the road, slumping in the gutter like a gunnysack filled only with bones.

Disturbed by the seemingly motionless frame in the near pitch-blackness of natural night, the pizza delivery man's co-worker worried that they had handled him too roughly: "Is he even breathing?"

Pulling a lighter from his back-pocket, the pizza delivery man knelt down beside the new guy; rolled him onto his back; and brought the weak flame up-close to reveal a hysterically blinking face contorted in pain: "He's fine – He's just a pussy."

Without extinguishing his nearly empty lighter, the pizza delivery man then stripped the new guy of his red leather satchel and coordinating baseball cap; brandished them before the reluctant and frightened young man like evidence of some crime or perversion; and calculatedly asked, "Where are your fucking stars now?" – At which point (almost on cue), the pizza delivery man's lighter dried-up and the actual stars overhead appeared like countless predators' eyes gazing down from tree perches, intimating a menace the new guy had never before clocked.

14.

In 1892, Oscar Wilde premiered his comedy of Victorian morals, **Lady Windermere's Fan**, in London's St. James Theatre. In the third act of this four act production, the character, Lord Darlington, famously quipped, "We are all in the gutter, but some of us are looking at the stars."

Of course, when the pizza delivery man asked the new guy lying in the gutter "Where are your fucking stars now?" he was referring to the celebrities about which the new guy hoped to write blogs professionally.

The actual stars overhead (not yet hidden behind the encroaching cumulonimbus clouds) were simply illustrative – In pitch-blackness; without even the weak, guttering flame of a disposable lighter, the pizza delivery man was challenging the new guy's perception – Having dragged him away from the artificial light emanating from the pizzeria's rear entrance, the pizza delivery man was showing the new guy that stars do not exist as projections upon a firmament encircling our planet: They are not within reach of the most sophisticated technologies but, rather, are billions and billions of miles away.

"Where are your fucking stars now?" was the pizza delivery man driving home to the new guy the fact that he was not going to be rescued from the gutter at that moment (or any moment) by his cultivated appreciation of luminous things filled with hot air.

Lying in the gutter, sucking wind for a punch to the gut that felt like a lead pipe; intimidated by two desperate and hostile men, the new guy contemplated the stars and, for their distance and ineffectuality, felt no consolation – Only a profound sense of emptiness: The absence of something within him to cultivate.

The predatory appearance of the stars was the new guy's acceptance of that fact: "I'm never gonna be a celebrity blogger, am I?"

15.

That same night, when his boss was alone in the pizzeria going through the till, the pizza delivery man entered through the carelessly, yet typically, unlocked rear entrance.

Having heard the latch click, his apprehensive boss reached for a dough-encrusted rolling pin, but relaxed when he saw that it was just the pizza delivery man: "Yeah, what do you want?"

Earlier, after having brought the new guy onboard, all three pizza delivery men had discussed exactly what they wanted – The pizza delivery man's co-worker insisted upon a health plan ("One that includes spouses and children"), while the new guy wanted a better hourly wage to compensate for those nights when customers did not tip. For the pizza delivery man, who still only wanted to find or make that something by which he would be judged important, it was enough to be entrusted as the embodiment of their expressed wishes: Their spokesman (even though he would never have admitted to this).

The three pizza delivery men settled upon two plans of action to achieve their aims: Plan A and Plan B.

Plan A involved a civil confrontation with their boss (that is, extrajudicial, but still in keeping with common decency) – Unfortunately, when the pizza delivery man opened his mouth to commence Plan A; when he first tried to represent his modest collective, he garbled his words, mispronouncing "aims".

"Alms?" his boss laughed. "You want to talk about alms? – Not even one week off, and you're already begging, [Pizza delivery man]?"

Disappointed in himself for having lost footing so early (for being made to feel like a mendicant gathering for the poor), the pizza delivery man sharply corrected: "No, [My boss], I want to talk about our union!"

At that point, like someone had shown him a picture of his daughter sucking-off a man of another race, the pizza delivery man's boss sat bolt upright from his tired slouch; leapt from the counter-top beside the till (his landing sending up a plume of flour from which his utterances would escape like pronouncements from on-high); and spoke: "Well, that's one of us, dickhead – You're fired."

Having anticipated that, the pizza delivery man (committed to the procedures laid out by Plan A) informed his imposing boss that all three of his delivery men were in the union.

Gripping the rolling pin in his hands; seeming to measure its weight and resilience the way gladiators once measured their weapons before their bloody contests, the pizza delivery man's boss rejoined, "Then it won't be difficult for you to pass on the good word: They're fired, too."

The pizza delivery man held his boss' eyes – Knowing that delivering pizzas, however modest, was still the only thing in which (or by which) he could find that something to make himself important, he knew he had to hold on: "[My co-worker] has a wife and kid" he began, but he was not permitted to finish.

His boss shouted him down: "Then he should've thought of that before he sent you in here!"

Following procedure; though laboring without expectation, the pizza delivery man tried to explain that without delivery men the pizzeria would grind to a halt: "You don't pull in enough off pick-ups; we're important to your business – You need us."

"I need you like I need another asshole!" countered his boss, who then rhetorically asked if his employee knew why pizza delivery men did not unionize: "Because you're a dime-a-fucking-dozen! I can't piss without hitting a monkey with a head to put a cap on; an arm to carry a pizza; and a car that'll last long enough 'till I replace him!

"Important to my fucking business? In the long run? - [Pizza delivery man], get the fuck out of here before I crack your fucking skull open!"

16.

Like a specialist law enforcement unit only missing German shepherds and guns (or a military reserve mustered to the aid of a flagging regiment), the pizza delivery man's co-worker and the new guy barged through the pizzeria's rear entrance seeking out their union's spokesman under-threat.

At the sight of them, their boss frantically waved about his rolling pin like an old man's cudgel for strays: "Stay the fuck back, you cock-suckers!" but like domesticated dogs let loose, deliriously feral, the two delivery men encroached without trepidation.

"I'm fucking warning you one last time! – Stay the fuck back or I'm calling the cops!"

It was when the pizza delivery man unplugged the wall-mounted phone behind him ("No one's calling the fucking cops!") that wires were first crossed – The pizza delivery man thought that he had only signaled that the time for civil negotiation was *almost* running out. For his co-worker, however, when the pizza delivery man prevented their boss from calling in a partial third-party mediator (the police) he was signaling that the time for civil negotiation had *already* run out.

Believing that Plan A had been scrapped in favor of Plan B, the pizza delivery man's co-worker showed no restraint when he threw blinding flour into his boss' face; stole the rolling pin from his flailing arm; and beat him within an inch of his life with it.

When the pizza delivery man shouted, "Don't fucking kill him!" his co-worker only thought, "This isn't the place" – He did not appreciate that, for the pizza delivery man, it was hopefully not yet the time, either.

17.

Pope Leo XIII's encyclical, **Rerum Novarum**, expressed truly beautiful sentiments:

> "The following duties bind the wealthy
> owner and the employer: not to look
> upon their work people as their
> bondsmen, but to respect in every man
> his dignity as a person ennobled by
> Christian character. They are reminded
> that, according to natural reason and
> Christian philosophy, working for gain
> is creditable, not shameful, to a man,
> since it enables him to earn an
> honorable livelihood; but to misuse
> men as though they were things in the
> pursuit of gain, or to value them solely
> for their physical powers - that is truly
> shameful and inhuman. Again justice
> demands that, in dealing with the

working man, religion and the good of
his soul must be kept in mind. Hence,
the employer is bound to see that the
worker has time for his religious
duties; that he be not exposed to
corrupting influences and dangerous
occasions; and that he be not led away
to neglect his home and family, or to
squander his earnings. Furthermore,
the employer must never tax his work
people beyond their strength, or
employ them in work unsuited to their
sex and age. His great and principal
duty is to give everyone what is just.
Doubtless, before deciding whether
wages are fair, many things have to be
considered; but wealthy owners and all
masters of labor should be mindful of
this - that to exercise pressure upon the
indigent and the destitute for the sake
of gain, and to gather one's profit out
of the need of another, is condemned

by all laws, human and divine. To defraud any one of wages that are his due is a great crime which cries to the avenging anger of Heaven. "Behold, the hire of the laborers... which by fraud has been kept back by you, crieth; and the cry of them hath entered into the ears of the Lord of Sabaoth.". Lastly, the rich must religiously refrain from cutting down the workmen's earnings, whether by force, by fraud, or by usurious dealing; and with all the greater reason because the laboring man is, as a rule, weak and unprotected, and because his slender means should in proportion to their scantiness be accounted sacred. *Were these precepts carefully obeyed and followed out, would they not be sufficient of themselves to keep under all strife and all its causes?"*

18.

Wishing that God had not permitted him to kill his boss; wishing that he did not have to ally himself with the Devil and a hash-abusing Congolese "freedom fighter" to achieve his earthly goal, the pizza delivery man turns the severed fingers over-and-over in his good hand, like rosary beads.

When he and his co-worker pull into the nearest 24-hour carwash, he has to excuse himself for a minute: "This whole business is giving me the squirts, and I need to wash the glass out of my hand. Yeah, I know - I'm a fucking 'tard."

Spotting a faded sign with directional arrow; pocketing his former employer's digits, he makes his way for the single-occupant restroom around back.

Closing the door; pulling hard on the handle to ensure it is locked, the pizza delivery man falls to his knees and prays before the altar-like sink, gripping its rim, searching for the reconciliation he has yet to find: "What the fuck, Man?"

Shaking, he leans forward over the lip of the sink; turns the faucet on; splashes cold water on his face and neck; and gently scrapes away the odd glass fragment from his cut hand.

In the sickly-lighting of the filthy carwash toilet; kneeling beside an un-flushed turd; peripherally aware of a wall-mounted condom dispenser, the pizza delivery man wonders if he should have just stayed with his co-worker, now elbow-deep in their dead boss' waste.

Finding this miserable space to be so much like the one he left behind (a steamed-up car filled with death, piss and shit), the pizza delivery man reaches from his supplicant's position and furiously slams the toilet bowl lid shut: "Who the fuck doesn't flush shit?"

For a moment, the pizza delivery man thinks about that simple rule: Flush shit – He thinks about the mothers and fathers the world-over who teach their children this rule.

He thinks about his own father.

19.

On December 7, 1965, Pope Paul VI proclaimed **Dignitatis Humanae** (or *Of the Dignity of the Human Person*). It was one of three Declarations made by the Second Ecumenical Council of the Vatican.

It read: "This Vatican Council declares that the human person has a right to religious freedom. This freedom means that all men are to be immune from coercion on the part of individuals or of social groups and of any human power, in such wise that no one is to be forced to act in a manner contrary to his own beliefs, whether privately or publicly, whether alone or in association with others, within due limits."

Because the pizza delivery man's father was a Traditionalist of that generation, he frequently told his son at the dinner table that the Declaration promulgated heresy and that the Second Vatican Council had "sold out and was playing grab-ass with other religions just to be popular."

Of course, the pizza delivery man's father did not object to religious freedom ("I'm a red-blooded American, for fuck's sake!") – He objected to the Declaration's de-emphasis of the most basic tenet of his faith: Jesus Christ's unique role in man's salvation.

Like other conservatives, the pizza delivery man's father resented *Dignitatis Humanae's* "1960's hippie-bullshit wording" ("The inquiry is to be free, carried on with the aid of teaching or instruction, communication and dialogue, in the course of which men explain to one another the truth they have discovered, or think they have discovered, in order thus to assist one another in the quest for truth") as if the Truth of Christ's victory on the cross was not a fact.

Were it not for his wife, the pizza delivery man's father would have joined the Sedevacantists: Traditionalist Catholics who believe the papal seat (the *sede*) is now vacant (*vacante*).

20.

Unexpectedly, the overhead ventilation fan in the carwash toilet whirs into life – The pizza delivery man knows that this is an uncommon occurrence – The decayed trim around the broken mirror; the crumbling tiles through which saturated insulation pokes; and the vine-like mold stains climbing the walls and ceiling indicate that this space rarely, if ever, gets a blast of fresh air.

In this neglected single-occupant restroom, the pizza delivery man, however, breathes easier for another reason: An unburdened conscience.

Staring into his fractured reflection in the mirror, the pizza delivery man says a prayer for his father: The man who told him to flush: The man who told him that even the Church compromised her principles to be relevant: The man who taught him that even the Church did what She had to do to be important.

PART IV.

1.

Jean-Luc Godard nailed it on the head – If you want to make popular entertainment then apply the formula sex and violence.

Because the Qur'an and the American author, James Salter, have said that the life of this world is but a sport and a pastime (an entertainment); if you want your life to be well-received, then you might also have to apply Godard's formula to it – In other words, if you want people to tune in to what you are doing, then you might have to be sexual and violent.

Unfortunately, sex and violence is not a chemical formula like H_2O; it is not that helpful. It is simpler, missing crucial detail – Unlike H_2O, it does not answer the critical question "What is the correct proportion between the two?"

Consequently, all aspiring men must decide for themselves how much sex and how much violence they will admit into their lives; which is problematic – If a man goes violently overboard, apportioning too little of his life to sex, then he runs the risk of alienating his audience.

Sex and violence is more a recipe than a formula – It leaves a bad taste in the mouth when one part outweighs the other by an undisclosed amount: That secret detail.

Because the Devil is in the details, a man who chooses not to consider the correct proportion of sex to violence in his work or life (simply because this proportion is a mystery) effectively chooses not to consider (not to grapple with) the Devil – This is dangerous.

Cursed are the immoderate.

"Open up!"

2.

Through the peephole, the pizza delivery man sees that it is not the police – He sighs in relief, yet still motions to his co-worker and the new guy not to make a sound.

Again, Robin Fletcher bangs on the apartment door: "Your car's out here – I know you're in there, so let's stop the games, okay?"

The kettle on the pizza delivery man's hotplate whistles – For a good minute, the sequestered delivery men stare intently at the traitorous metal pot before the pizza delivery man lifts it from the burner; hands it to his co-worker ("This better be good fucking coffee."); and then answers the door: "Yeah, and what do you want?"

Through the very slight crack, Fletcher inserts his face like the old hand that he is and answers, "You, pizza boy – I want you."

Furtively casting his eyes up and down the hallway, the pizza delivery man says that he cannot honestly understand why: "Dude, I'm yesterday's news – I'm just an old story."

He tries to end the conversation (literally, close the door on the unwelcome interlocution), but the *paparazzo* jams his foot in the way: "Sometimes, pizza boy, old stories find new legs: Second wind: Fresh blood."

That last figure of speech reminds the pizza delivery man of a parasite: A tick or a leech – He almost says as much, but he is interrupted.

139

Fletcher holds up the day's newspaper: "Your boss is dead."

Sticking his head further into the pizza delivery man's apartment; registering the effect of his announcement on the face of the pizza delivery man's co-worker (as the new guy is hidden in shadow), Fletcher asks why the two of them are not at work.

In a voice twisted to a strange, unrecognizable falsetto register by nerves, the new guy pipes up revealing his presence and more: "The pizzeria's closed 'till his replacement from corporate shows up tomorrow, is all!"

The pizza delivery man shoots a sideways glance at his co-worker, as if to say "Shut him the fuck up before he says anything stupid!" – He then grabs the newspaper from Fletcher's hand and reads the caption beneath his former employer's photograph: "What are you retarded? Our boss is missing – There's a big fucking difference."

Ignoring the pizzeria's invisible third employee; unctuously, Fletcher encourages the pizza delivery man's optimism: "That's good, pizza boy.

Keep hope alive, or some shit like that, right? - Have the cops stopped by to ask you guys any questions?"

Gritting his teeth, the pizza delivery man pulls hard, slamming the door on the *paparazzo's* foot: "Bitch, just fuck off already!"

Squeezing his under-developed shoulder into the narrow crack, Robin Fletcher digs deep and pushes back into the door, resisting closure.

Feigning offense, though actually hurt, he asks the pizza delivery man why he insists on being such a prick: "When I only came here to apologize!"

"Apologize?" huffs the pizza delivery man, staring distractedly at his co-worker and the new guy sipping their coffees while he struggles. "What the hell for?"

The door pinches too hard on the *paparazzo's* chest, pinning the surface-mounted deadbolt into his back – Squirming, he answers, "For [Madame Bardot]. Maybe I was wrong – Maybe it wasn't an accident."

The pizza delivery man considers Fletcher's admission – The unexpected, yet welcome, vindication softens him; he considers letting go of the door's dummy-knob, perhaps even inviting the bastard inside: "So what are you telling me? You accept that it was self-defense?"

Feeling the sharp edge of a deadbolt cutting surprisingly deep into his shoulder-blade, Robin Fletcher grimaces: "No, I don't – I think you just fucking snapped."

At that, the pizza delivery man kicks the *paparazzo* in the ribs, simultaneously letting go of his apartment door, sending him sprawling to the hallway's damp, moldy carpet.

3.

When a man snaps, he goes crazy.

Smug college students like to say that craziness does not exist. They like to say that it is relative and that what is crazy for one person is perfectly sane for another, but smug college students are young and do not know how to kick around ideas without picking them up – Like children with mittens bought by mom, they pick up garbage and dead birds and take them home when they should not.

Because most people the world over think that it is crazy to put your hand in an operating blender because a dog commands you (even if it is a great dog with a gift for gab), craziness is real.

If a man puts his hand into a food processor's spinning blades because a charismatic dog said so, then that man is not seeing the world differently like a poet – That man is just not seeing the world at all; he is blind.

Because the pizza delivery man has always thought it was crazy to put a hand in a blender because a charming dog says so, he knows that he is sane.

4.

According to the American author, Mike Godwin, the longer an internet discussion lasts the more likely it is that one of the participants will attack another by comparing his or her position to one held by the Nazis or Adolf Hitler – This amusing observation is called Godwin's Law.

When debating the existence of craziness, a similar law seems to apply.

When debating the existence of craziness (if given enough time) invariably someone will reference Muslim suicide bombers: Men and women who, for all intents and purposes, throw their entire bodies into blenders: "And what about them, huh? What you call crazy, they call perfectly sane – Man, why can't your generation see that it's all a matter of fucking opinion?"

Too often the person making that point is a smug college student waiting for his next bong hit.

(As much as it hurts) in defense of that smug prick, he resists acknowledging the existence of craziness because his culture has been careless with its application – Westerners throw around "You're crazy!" with the same lack of consideration they give to the phrase "I love you".

If only to stop stoned college students from talking damned nonsense, Muslim suicide bombers' must not be mislabeled as crazy – They must be rightly recognized as sane men existing with us on a value-laden continuum of comprehensibility, by which their beliefs and grievances (and inspired

144

actions) find comprehension and forgiveness *after* ours.

5.

Sane people disagree, and the points on which they disagree ("Is it crazy to stick my hand in a blender if I am retrieving a baby that was put there?" or "Is it crazy to explode myself in a crowded mall in defense of Allah?") are not evidence of the others' insanity – The points on which sane people disagree are only proof that sanity is just the objective lens through which human beings see the world telescopically.

Like an early seventeenth century Dutch refracting telescope (the type Galileo later used for his famous observations about our solar system's real heliocentric configuration), human vision requires something like an objective and an ocular lens.

For the sake of illustration, imagine that the human lenses are both housed in a cylindrical chamber pointed at the moon, like a Galilean telescope.

The human being's objective lens (that lens nearest the moon) is its sanity – It gathers reflected sunlight from the lunar surface and sends the uncorrupted crater-filled image into the body of the telescope toward the human being's ocular lens: That lens nearest the heart and mind.

The human being's ocular lens is that lens with which he has the power to change his relationship with the focal point of the objective – It is that lens with which a man can choose to see the world more clearly or (if he desires) blur it until our solar system appears to revolve around the Earth.

6.

Although all unimportant men must choose between guaranteed suffocation at the hands of a disappointed and maternal gorilla or an uncertain rebellion led by a hash-smoking "freedom fighter", most men (important and unimportant alike) cannot see this choice.

Because most unimportant men cannot see this choice, most of them asphyxiate to death.

Because the pizza delivery man in this "life-never-to-be-lived" can see this choice, it can be said that his ocular lens setting affords him a sharper image of the world than that possessed by most everyone – For this, being closer to seeing true sanity than almost anyone alive, the pizza delivery man believes that his atrocities (killing "Madame Bardot" and his boss) put him on the value-laden continuum of comprehensibility *before* both Muslim suicide bombers and the entire West.

If only the Occidental and Oriental could see his vision for themselves.

7.

For the pizza delivery man, his new sense of being the sanest man alive makes the threat of being stigmatized insane a particularly difficult pill to swallow: A real kick in the balls.

He nearly disbelieves it: "I'm the one who sees the world more clearly, so how can my tweaking of this shithole planet (however violent) be less forgivable? – Fucking hell!"

When the pizza delivery man booted Robin Fletcher in the ribs ("Fucking cunt rag!"), he did so because he recognized that the *paparazzo* might be a harbinger of unwelcome things to come – He might be the first in a long line of people to dismiss the pizza delivery man's demand for importance and serious consideration as the ranting of a lunatic.

Because being a lunatic is like being a child (both are not moral agents capable of acting with respect to right and wrong), saying that a man suffers from lunacy infantilizes him.

Being called "loony" (especially by the community at large) would turn the pizza delivery man into a pizza boy without an objective lens: A blind pizza boy – Which would suck.
8.

In the *paparazzo's* assessment ("I think you just fucking snapped."), the pizza delivery man heard the lock in the door leading to civil society turning, threatening to shut him out forever.

In his mind's ear, he imagined voices: "Oh that? That's just the crazy pizza boy who killed

[Madame Bardot] before he killed his boss – And all for no good reason!"

Although the pizza delivery man knows that he is sane, he also knows that he must play the odds – It is very likely that people will question his sanity when the *paparazzo's* speculative "reporting" hits the internet; this is something against which he cannot fight, something that he cannot ignore.

Accepting that; with a new fire under his ass, the pizza delivery man kicked Robin Fletcher to the moldy hallway carpet because he immediately wanted to get to work making himself into that acceptable and important crazy man: An eccentric: A crazy man who gets the job done.

9.

With the *paparazzo* outside of their private space, the delivery men continue with their meeting, aware of their spokesman's new irrepressible sense of urgency.

Sitting cross-legged, the pizza delivery man's co-worker tries to loosen him up – He hands him a mug filled with coffee: "You're out of milk."

Because the pizza delivery man is always out of milk; because he has other concerns at the moment, he takes his coffee black: "Forget about it – [New guy], hand me the sugar?"

When he reaches for the last packet of sugar the pizza delivery man filched from Starbucks, the new guy accidentally knocks over a shoebox – Out of which falls a grimy plastic bag filled with congealed blood and his dead boss' four severed digits.

Because the new guy has not seen the disembodied fingers before, the pizza delivery man has to ask him again: "The sugar?"

Even though he is shocked and hyperventilating, the new guy manages to keep it together long enough to hand over the last sugar packet. Unfortunately, though trying not to lose it, like a doe shivering in the forest underbrush, he still draws attention and fire from the pizza delivery man's co-worker under incredible stress for his filial responsibilities - Like buckshot ripping through game, his accusation makes a bloody mess of the new guy: "You didn't fucking do it, did you?"

Defensively, the new guy stammers, "What the fuck are you talking about?"

Wiping spit from the crease in his lip, the pizza delivery man's co-worker growls, "Your fucking job, that's what – They're not coming, are they?"

Measuring the situation; feeling like he is watching the new guy frantically pull his entrails, like sausage links, back into his abdomen, the pizza delivery man steps in before it really gets out of control: "Settle the fuck down!"

He pushes his co-worker back: "I said settle the fuck down!"

Nearly in tears, the new guy screams, "I did my fucking job! All three pizzerias – Almost got my ass handed to me, but I did my fucking job, you prick!"

At this point, the pizza delivery man turns on him, too: "What do you mean you almost got your ass handed to you?"

Speechless, the new guy's reddening eyes widen imploringly.

Rejoining the interrogation he initiated, the pizza delivery man's co-worker shoves the young delivery man against the apartment wall: "What the fuck did you tell them?"

Regaining his voice, the new guy meekly insists that he told them only what he had been coached to tell them: "But one of the fucking managers – Shit, I don't know how long he was there, listening-"

Viciously, the pizza delivery man's co-worker backhands the new guy: "Don't fucking lie to me! Nothing you were told to reveal to them could've gotten your ass beat – What did you say?"

Broken down into tears, yet still coherent, the new guy confesses that he might have said something to the effect of "We're finally gonna get ours" - But nothing more than that.

"Ours?"

A pall falls on the pizza delivery man and his co-worker.

Slumping onto his bean bag chair; forcing pellets from out of the frayed seams, the pizza delivery man slowly draws his hand across his face: "Ours? Motherfucker, they don't want us to have anything."

The new guy sobs: "Come on, [Pizza delivery man], that fucking asshole didn't know what I was talking about – He just wanted me out of his kitchen. Look, they got the address. They got the time. They got the message. Three pizzerias. Three delivery men-"

"That's including the guy you were talking to when you almost got your ass done?"

"Yes – They'll all be there."

Looking over at his co-worker, the pizza delivery man asks, "But are they gonna be alone?" before he quietly considers how best to roll with the punches, before he wonders if life has finally given him a lucky break.

10.

Remember a homeless man.

Now, think of that homeless man having unprotected sex with a woman.

Is that thought uncomfortable?

Does the thought of a homeless man having unprotected sex with a woman disgust you? Does it bring to mind diseases? Do you strongly suspect that sexually transmitted diseases infect your homeless man?

Admittedly, you are not likely worried about the homeless man contracting a disease from a woman – Which raises the question: If not from a woman, then from whom has your homeless man contracted an STD?

Another man?

Possibly.

Perhaps the homeless man you remembered was a drug addict, too – In this case, he might be a carrier of some pathogen he received from a contaminated needle.

Assume, however, that your homeless man was neither a homosexual practicing unsafe sex nor an intravenous drug user – From whom would he then have contracted an STD?

Even though it is not likely that a healthy woman would have sex with a homeless man (healthy women have sex with strangers from clubs and bars); in the event that one did, does it not seem that the homeless man for whom his sexual history is probably ancient history risks infection more?

11.

For better or worse, homeless men are "Dirty" in the West – Because sexually transmitted diseases are also "Dirty", the human mind lumps both of them together in the same mental compartment.

Unfortunately for a homeless man; when asked to retrieve a memory of him, the mind cannot help but withdraw notions of Syphilis, Gonorrhea, Chlamydia or something of this kind – As a consequence of mental associations, STDs infect homeless men (even those who have never had the pleasure of unprotected sex): "Poor bastards."

12.

Homeless men are unimportant men.

They have that type of unimportance that makes them obstacles to be hurriedly walked around or stepped over as if they suffered from a particularly virulent strain of a disease.

It is reasonable to suspect that homeless men are dirty because they are unimportant – After all, a family made homeless after a natural disaster does not become an unimportant family; they do not become dirty because they do not own a house.

Sound deductive reasoning might then argue, "Because all unimportant men are dirty men; because pizza delivery men are unimportant men, all pizza delivery men are dirty men." – It might also deduce that because all pizza delivery men are dirty men; because the mind infects the dirty man with communicable diseases, all pizza delivery men seem (in the mind's eye) to carry diseases.

In that way, delivering pizzas is like being a leper.

Because leprous men were historically quarantined in colonies against their will, it has always taken authority to bring them together – In the absence of authority, the pizza delivery man assembled the three delivery men from their respective pizzerias with the promise of love.

PART V.

1.

The word "Abattoir" is a misleading word –
An abattoir sounds like a place where elderly couples
spend weekday afternoons strolling around exotic
plants; where teachers bring their young students to
see butterflies; or to where women excuse themselves
when they need to "powder their noses".

The word "Abattoir" sounds so much like the
word "Boudoir" (a woman's private room where
anything might happen) that the three delivery men
invited to attend a meeting at the local abattoir might
be forgiven for being pissed to find that it is nothing
like a whorehouse.

"What the fuck?"

An abattoir is a slaughterhouse – It is a place
where animals are stunned, hung upside down, and
bled to death for food and other products.

"Where's the pussy? – Man, I thought there
was gonna be pussy here."

"That kid said this was an abattoir, right?"

While the pizza delivery man explains from a chair leaning against the opposite wall that there must have been a misunderstanding ("An abattoir is not a bordello."); while he explains that the onus for the three delivery men having arrived at a slaughterhouse rests firmly with them, the new guy quietly moves to lock them all inside, preventing any escape.

Once the only exit is sealed, the pizza delivery man's co-worker (waiting on an elevated walkway directly above the three bitterly disappointed delivery men) receives the signal to cut the lights – In pitch blackness, he overturns the large industrial drum beside him, pouring gallons of gasoline upon the panicked men below.

"Jesus, what the fuck is going on?!"

From his seat against the opposite wall, the pizza delivery man runs at the three men with a new disposable lighter in hand, screaming at the top of his lungs, "Do you bitches want to burn?"

Were it not the for the new guy (shrouded in darkness) prodding the three flammable men from behind with a broom handle, they would all have high-tailed it back in the direction of the slaughterhouse's entrance – However, corralled like cattle, they are forced to face the shrieking, ghostly, seemingly decapitated head of the pizza delivery man lit by a single flame, levitating before them.

"Do you bitches want to burn?"

Because none of the three petrol-doused men want to be set on fire, they all throw their hands up before the floating, incendiary face, crying, "No! God, no!"

From his perch near the rafters, the pizza delivery man's co-worker shouts down, "Then shut the fuck up!" – His voice echoes in the desolate and cavernous slaughterhouse.

Immediately, the three delivery men fall silent, cowering together (each groping for the hand of another) – They all know the rules: Pizza delivery men are killed for one of three reasons.

On tenterhooks; their nerves stretched to their limits, they wait to find out whether they are being murdered for thrills, murdered for a little money, or murdered for a combination of the two.

When the pizza delivery man extinguishes his lighter, all three drenched delivery men suspect that they are being toyed with and are in for a long and tortuous night.

"They're doing this for the thrill," they think.

Sickened by gasoline fumes and anxiety, one of them dry heaves before predictably begging for mercy from the man who holds his life in his hand: "Please, don't kill me."

Though moved, the pizza delivery man knows that he must hold the line – He knows that he must persist with the threat of immolation.

"It's for their good, too" he reminds himself

2.

The pizza delivery man feels like Moses fighting for the freedom of his people – Only his people (his slaves) are the master's unrecognized bastards waiting for the legitimation that will never come, resisting their own liberation for this misapprehension.

3.

The sound of steady dripping from the holding pens that had been power-washed earlier, like that from stalactites, contributes to the cave-like feel of the slaughterhouse.

Drenched in refined crude; still hours away from sunlight, the three captive delivery men are like unlucky spelunkers who have fallen into the very bowels of the Earth where no one can help them.

Already petrol vapors affect their nervous systems – The three sway, struggling to remain upright, like street people high on inhaling aerosol can propellants.

One of them pleads for ventilation, but he is met by a wall of black silence (and a sharp, rib-directed jab from behind from what feels like a broom handle).

Dizzy, the three begin to flop over their haunches, gripping their upper-thighs for support to prevent them from falling to their knees (their torsos as listless as a paralytic's legs) – Eventually, however, they fall.

It is the sound of their bodies slumping to the slaughterhouse floor that tells the pizza delivery man that it is time. He orders the lights to be turned back on and the hose with which the pens are cleaned to be fetched.

When the new guy returns with nozzle in hand, the pizza delivery man instructs him to thoroughly wash the three human wicks: "Sober these fuckers up before they die."

4.

When "Madame Bardot" last leveled her gun at the real pizza delivery man, she did so at close-range: Execution style.

"Like in the movies," she thought.

When she did that, the real pizza delivery man's body responded naturally – It released epinephrine (otherwise known as adrenaline) which readied him for strenuous physical activity.

With the bio-chemical resources to perform at his (admittedly modest) peak, the real pizza delivery man could have fought or he could have fled.

Because he did not think he could wrestle both the gun and his life from "Madame Bardot's" hands, the real pizza delivery man chose not to fight.

Because he did not think he could outrun a bullet (even one fired from a likely inaccurate "Saturday Night Special"), the real pizza delivery man resisted the temptation to run.

Unable to save himself within the "Fight-or-Flight" dichotomy, the real pizza delivery man briefly thought that the epinephrine might have improved his powers of speech.

Remember: He barked, "No" - Which was not an improvement.

Barking "No" only convinced "Madame Bardot" to pull the trigger.

In the brief moments between that unhelpful outburst and his death, the real pizza delivery man directed his body's energies to one last desperate attempt to save himself – He augmented his faith in human goodness: A goodness that respects a man's life when it recognizes his simple biological capacity.

In the last refuge of the condemned (fortified by his body's epinephrine), the pizza delivery man waited for the storm of "Madame Bardot" to subside and for her to be embarrassed by her lapse in humanity.

He should have tried something else.

5.

The pizza delivery man of this "life-never-to-be-lived" (who believes that he survived "Madame Bardot" only because he fought back in self-defense) knows as well as the real pizza delivery man that faith in human goodness is suicidal.

Knowing that faith in human goodness is suicidal, the pizza delivery man of this "life-never-to-be-lived" cannot begin to imagine a fraternal union with each delivery man considering the interests of the others, like a brother.

Unable to appeal to human goodness, the pizza delivery man (like a good Christian wishing to avoid obvious violence) would have liked to have given the delivery men something to earn their membership in the union: Something like the promise of a better life

Unfortunately, the pizza delivery man has known that he cannot promise a better life that does not require the delivery men to accept that they are delivery men – He has known that he cannot offer a better life through the union without first destroying each man's delusion (that thing he believes himself really to be; that thing that frustrates identification with other "lepers").

The pizza delivery man cannot attack all of them with the same foreknowledge with which he attacked the new guy under the stars, crippling his dream to be a celebrity blogger.

Neither can he find with them that common ground by which he secured his co-worker's union membership – Not all delivery men want health benefits (especially not those that do not envision themselves delivering pizza pies for much longer).

When the pizza delivery man conceived Plan B, he considered all of those limitations.

Unable to galvanize his colleagues peacefully; uneager to commit another act of obvious violence like that perpetrated against his former boss, the pizza delivery man designed the slaughterhouse part of Plan B around "non-violence": That resistance that alleviates the conscience while still permitting a man to seriously fuck with people: That violence that does not get the hands dirty.

6.

On August 29th, 1931, Mahatma Gandhi (one of the great proponents of "non-violence") sailed for England.

Because he had long been advocating Indian self-sufficiency and the boycott of foreign (particularly British) made cloth, Lancashire textile industrialists and trade unions invited him to their region to witness first-hand the devastation India's "non-cooperation" was causing.

Since the 1800's, Lancashire (a county in the North West of the country) had been known for its wealthy textile manufacturing; however, after the First World War, this industry had been in marked decline: A decline which many astute insiders attributed in some way to Indian nationalists refusing to buy their goods.

In the spring of 1931; in the large Lancashire town of Blackburn, nearly ten thousand people assembled, calling upon their government to save them – The minute book of the Blackburn District Cotton Employers' Association reads, "Unless a firm stand is taken which will stamp out Sedition, Lawlessness and Disorder [in India], there can be no hope for a revival of the Lancashire Cotton Trade."

In such an atmosphere, when William L. Shirer (an American journalist who accompanied Gandhi on his trip through Depression-struck England) reported that the textile workers gave Mr. Gandhi a "tumultuous welcome", it can be said that he was reporting only half of the story – When writing about men who espouse "non-violence", it is tempting to turn hagiographer – Shirer's account gives the impression that all of struggling Lancashire stood in solidarity with the Indian independence movement even against its own interests; which, of course, could not be true.

Irina Spector-Marks in her paper, *"Mr. Gandhi Visits Lancashire: A Study in Imperial Miscommunication" (2008)*, provides the missing half to the story of Gandhi's "tumultuous welcome" – In words that are not Ms. Spector-Marks': The Lancashire textile industry (comprised of trade unionists and owners) believed that Gandhi had arrived (like the genial, Christ-like sage he was purported to be) to listen to their woes and to capitulate, ending the Indians' boycott and returning their county to its former glory.

In short-hand, Gandhi received a "tumultuous welcome" because he came bearing all of the hallmarks of the Messiah come to deliver Lancashire's poor.

But Gandhi did not journey to Lancashire to deliver himself and his people like paschal lambs – He came to explain the boycott and to leave.

Through Gandhi's championing of "non-violence", India was victorious in its quest for independence – However, because all victors require a vanquished, the story of India's "non-violent" revolution (like the story of Gandhi's warm reception) is incomplete: Half-true.

The missing half of the story of Gandhi's "non-violence" is the story of a former cotton-mill laborer in Depression-Era England – Generally treated as dumb (that is, mute) this former laborer once found his voice standing shoulder-to-shoulder with his fellow co-workers (nearly ten thousand strong) only to have it drowned out by the moral legalese of a self-righteous, homespun wearing killer who had tricked the world's intellectuals into believing that starving an unemployed Englishman's child in a cramped and cold tenement (in a country whose national insurance plan had turned into dust after the bitterest war) was not really an act of violence: "After all, a malnourished English child is not malnourished; it is English – This is simple logic."

7.

Pacing along the elevated walkway of the slaughterhouse, the pizza delivery man shouts down,

"Be sure to wash their eyes, [New guy]! I don't want anyone going blind! – They're no good if they're blind."

When he reaches his co-worker leaning against the railing (surveying the scene below), he engages him in light conversation, challenging him to imagine the abattoir filled with dung-dropping, cud-chewing animals: "If you squint and pretend that the three guys down there getting power-washed are cows or something, you get the feeling of being here during the day – This place has gotta be wild."

Harassed by the prospect of getting caught, the pizza delivery man's co-worker has no patience for idle talk: "[The new guy] fucked up. We both know that. We can wash these cunts somewhere else. We've done what we came to do; we put the fear of something like God in them – So let's get fucking gone before that eavesdropping bitch manager and whoever else gets here!"

Though the pizza delivery man appreciates his co-worker's concerns, he does not immediately respond to them – He is too distracted by the

Congolese "freedom fighter" beneath them, stumbling around the still-flammable delivery men with a lit joint dangling from his mouth and an automatic rifle sliding off his shoulder like a bra-strap.

To the pizza delivery man, the "freedom fighter" looks more like a prison queen admiring prospective bitches than a commander inspecting the *Ilungas* he should hope to mold into men.

When the pizza delivery man finally says something, he does not seem to address what troubles his co-worker – Instead, he asks him if he is afraid: "More to the point – Are you afraid of me?"

Feeling his head throb, the pizza delivery man's co-worker remembers the thrashing he received from the pizza delivery man when he was jumped in the abandoned construction site; and then he honestly answers, "No, I'm not afraid of you – But what's that gotta do with getting the hell out of here?"

The pizza delivery man spits – He watches his spit hit the slaughterhouse floor, stained with decades of dried, bovine blood.

As if he were thinking aloud, the pizza delivery man asks his co-worker if he believes the new guy fears him: "Because I think he's more afraid of being a nobody than he is of me: More afraid of not hanging out with celebrities."

The pizza delivery man's co-worker shrugs his shoulders: "Yeah, that's probably true – So what?"

"And what about those guys down there?" asks the pizza delivery man, pointing towards the three men he only moments ago imagined to be dumb animals fated for the rendering plant. "You think those guys shivering in their piss-soaked pants are any different? – You think they're afraid of me? Afraid of us?"

The pizza delivery man's co-worker answers that he does: "We dropped gallons of gasoline on them and threatened to set them on fire – They're fucking terrified, trust me."

It is all the pizza delivery man can do not to spit in his co-worker's face: "I do trust you, but if we let them go now they're going straight to the cops."

That disclosure, unexpected like a baby lost in the third trimester, shocks and disgusts the pizza delivery man's co-worker – He rages: "Motherfucker? What the fuck did we go through all this trouble for?" before he lowers his voice: "Are you telling me we're gonna have to kill these cock-suckers, too?"

Again, the Congolese "freedom fighter" grabs the pizza delivery man's focus – That stoned bastard is dancing around the slaughterhouse floor like an attention seeking teenage girl, cradling his rifle as if it were a nursing baby.

8.

Because the pizza delivery man still does not have a talent for anything (including leadership), Plan B had a serious design flaw of which the pizza delivery man was aware.

All along, the pizza delivery man has known that he would not be able to command the three petrol-doused men when they are out of his sight ("Out of sight and out of mind."). He has known that because he has known that his very modest authority (that is, his ability to instill fear) is limited to each act of violence he commits – He does not have the law's reputation for reprisal: Its awesome power that stretches beyond its reach like a mother's.

Nothing outstrips a mother's coercion.

In fact, when the pizza delivery man told his co-worker that the three delivery men would snitch to the cops, he had the mental image of a mother's favorite child turning tattle-tale, reporting its rebellious sibling for some act of which both mom and favorite child disapprove.

Like an effete, milk-wet boy siding with his mother, when a man aligns his interests with the law, he almost guarantees himself victory – So, naturally, the delivery men when freed would go to the cops.

Because he is not the empowering law; because he is not the source of nutrient-rich, muscle-and-bone-growing breast milk, the pizza delivery man has known that to win the hearts and minds of the three gasoline-covered delivery men would require him to reconceive "Mom" for them – To do this, he has known that he would need a lucky break: A miracle.

The new guy's fuck up was that miracle.

9.

Breast milk can transmit more than nutrients to a child. It can also transmit disease – Because of the high incidence of HIV infection in the Congo, if the Congolese "freedom fighter" were a woman nursing a real baby (rather than an automatic rifle), he might be infecting it with HIV.

Being incapable of empowering the three gasoline-soaked delivery men with anything matching the law's authority; like a possessive sibling wanting to replace "Mom" and forge an unbreakable bond with her other children (knowing that he does not have the goodness of her breast), the pizza delivery man plans to point-out the diseases in her milk.

Like a boy with a peculiar psycho-sexual development, (in order to become "Mom") the pizza delivery man intends to infect his brothers with fear: The fear that their mother's nourishing milk is deadly, too – Which is the fear of unimportant men in revolt.

"[Pizza delivery man], the fuckers just pulled into the parking lot! – What the fuck are we gonna do?"

10.

"Take it!"

The delivery man who had earlier pled for his life after dry-heaving now begs not to have to take it: "Please, don't, I don't understand-"

"Take it, you lousy shit queer!"

The dry-heaver takes the severed finger being handed to him.

"Now put it in your fucking pocket! I said put it in your pocket! – And don't let me see you take it out!"

The other two gasoline-drenched delivery men are each handed a finger with similar orders.

"Eyes up here, ladies! Now, ask yourselves 'When those doors open are they gonna believe me when I tell them I had nothing doing with the dead manager over at [The pizza delivery man's pizzeria]?' – The fuck they are!

176

"You're pizza boys, for fuck's sake! – Perverts by trade."

The pizza delivery man squats down and gets right in the face of the pudgy delivery man with tears in his eyes for the ordeal and the fumes: "And you thought you were gonna fucking rat on us?"

"What?"

"You thought you were just gonna fucking ride this out, and then go to the cops?"

The tearful delivery man whips his head from side-to-side, shaking his fleshy jowls: "No, no, God, I never thought that–"

"Shut the fuck up! – I know what you were thinking!"

At first bawling unintelligibly, the tearful delivery man eventually screams, "I just wanted not to die! I just wanted not to die!"

The pizza delivery man's co-worker, manning the front entrance, shoots back a look that says "That was way too fucking loud, man".

The pizza delivery man smacks the crybaby upside the head: "Bitch, don't you fucking scream like that again! Do as I say - March out the backdoor with us and none of you cunts are gonna die today.

"But if you stay here? With them? They're gonna break down that fucking door – And you!"

"Me?"

"Pretty boy, they're gonna fuck you twelve ways to Sunday for that pretty face."

The pretty boy is not that pretty. Being pretty is a gift with which you are born; it is a talent for pleasing people with a smile – The pretty boy is only marginally better looking than the others.

"[Pizza delivery man], they're trying to break down the door! – Christ, that fucker actually brought the cops!"

"[New guy], unlock the backdoor! – Do it!"

The pizza delivery man turns from the new guy sprinting a bee-line to the rear entrance back to the three terrified delivery men collectively shitting it: "Listen to me! Listen to me! – Right now your only crime is trespassing (if those cock-suckers outside could even prove you were here) – But if you get caught with us and those fucking fingers in your pocket, you're all going down for murder – It's your choice: Leave with us now and maybe get a slap on the wrist for being here when you shouldn't have; or stay and get a thick cock up your ass in the prison shower every day for the rest of your life!"

11.

Is it wrong to infect a man with fear?

Is it wrong to wean him from his mother?

Is it wrong to demand that he grow up, especially if that man's retarded maturation prevents another from achieving that something by which he will be important: Complete manhood?

Is it wrong to play God?

12.

In the 1986 World Cup, Argentine soccer player, Diego Maradona, scored two goals in a match against England. Though his second goal is recognized as the "Goal of the Century", his first goal is far more ignominious – It was scored off an illegal handball.

To the anger of English supporters (and believers in fair-play), the referee allowed it.

That year, Argentina went on to win the World cup with Maradona taking top individual honor.

When asked about the illegal handball, Maradona evasively answered that it was "The hand of God".

It was twenty years before he confessed to something the whole world had been replaying for decades – It was twenty years before that cocaine-addicted Argentine came clean.

All men play at being God – Some men just get to keep the trophy.

14.

"You gotta smoke that in here?"

The Congolese "freedom fighter" answers, "Yeah, I do gotta smoke this in here."

Choosing to ignore the hash-and-cannabis-bud joint burning in his small studio apartment, the pizza delivery man tells the three men still reeking of gasoline to remove their soaked jeans ("Leaving the fingers in the pockets.") and to take turns washing-off in his cramped shower ("Do I look like I give a fuck that there's no fucking water pressure?").

"[New guy], there are some Denny's salt shakers in the top drawer there – Give them all a handful of salt to rub the gas off with."

After the three are washed, the pizza delivery man gives each a pair of his own pants – To the crybaby (who is fat), he offers a choice between a pair of shorts and a pair of sweat pants: "With scissors, if you need to cut the waistband."

When they are dressed, the pizza delivery man explains the situation: "You're not getting your pants back, so forget about it – We're gonna hold on to them."

The dry-heaver wants to know "What for?"

Authoritatively, the pizza delivery man answers, "Cause they're your pants with your ball hairs; your piss stains; your dried cum; your DNA; and your prints all over our dead boss' fingers – In case you change your mind about going to the cops."

The three, newly complicit delivery men feel their guts drop like they are in a free-falling elevator.

The pizza delivery man's co-worker tells the pretty boy to stop rubbing his eyes: "You're not dreaming, asshole."

The pretty boy says that he knows that: "My eyes are just burning still for the gas you fuckers poured on us – 'Sides, in my dreams, I'm usually doing this housewife I deliver pizzas to."

Seizing the moment, the pizza delivery man announces that it is time for all six of them to make their dreams come true.

PART VI.

1.

"Was it you at the slaughterhouse?"

Robin Fletcher shoves his recorder into the pizza delivery man's face, following him as he walks hurriedly across the pizzeria's parking lot to work.

The pizza delivery man says that he does not know about what the *paparazzo* is talking.

Squinting, as if to say "Whatever, man – I'll play along", Fletcher describes what happened the night before at the abattoir: "It seems a few pizza boys broke into it for a meeting or something. Hell, maybe they were just sucking each other off (I don't know), but somehow the cops caught wind of it-"

"Any arrests?"

Insulted by the pizza delivery man's weak charade, Fletcher refuses to answer that question: "From what I'm told, there was gasoline all over the place, like the pizza boys were gonna burn the slaughterhouse down."

Cocking his head to the side; trying to see the pizza delivery man from a different angle, the *paparazzo* asks him a very unexpected question: "Pizza boy, are you some kind of militant animal rights activist?"

The pizza delivery man immediately turns, charges Fletcher and grabs him by the collar: "Tit-for-tat, asshole! I'll answer your question, if you answer mine – Do the cops know the delivery men who were at the slaughterhouse?"

Appreciating that he cannot weasel his way out of this, the *paparazzo* answers, "No, they only got suspicions cause of what the guy who tipped them off said."

Contemptuously, the pizza delivery man reminds the *paparazzo* of what he earlier told him: "*Somehow* the cops caught wind of it?"

Breaking free of the pizza delivery man's grip, Fletcher indignantly claims that he does not have to tell him "every little fucking thing!" before adding, "Now, it's your turn, dickhead!"

Simultaneously, in the brief moment that the pizza delivery man considers the question "Are you some kind of militant animal rights activist?" he spies (for the first time) through the pizzeria's front glass windows the new manager from corporate.

Fletcher comments that she is quite a looker before he insists that the pizza delivery man fulfill his side of the bargain: "Are you a fucking militant animal rights activist?"

Because the last good-looking woman in his life mistook him for a mule, the pizza delivery man begrudgingly answers, "Yeah, probably – But I've never tried to burn down a fucking slaughterhouse!"

2.

After the pizzeria stops taking orders for the night; after the front-doors are locked and the metal-grating pulled down; after his co-worker and the new guy have left to loiter in the parking lot, the pizza delivery man approaches the good-looking manager from corporate (the woman who earlier gave him a free Super-sized Coca-Cola because he looked like he could use it).

Without saying a word, like a man who is only searching for his apartment keys, the pizza delivery man reaches into his pocket and pulls out a napkin in which he has wrapped one of his dead boss' severed fingers.

Placing it on the good-looking manager's desk, he patiently waits for her to take notice – At the moment, she is busily inputting data into a computer spreadsheet, mumbling about how she cannot imagine a world without computers and how grateful she is that the ledger book is a thing of the past.

When the good-looking manager finally takes notice of the pizza delivery man's gift, she thinks it is just this: A gift - As an attractive woman, she is used to unwelcome attention.

Because she is his boss for the time being, she forces herself to be more considerate of the pizza delivery man's feelings than she would normally be: "Oh, what's this?"

Because she is accustomed to taking charge, she does not wait for the pizza delivery man to answer – She managerially opens the napkin.

The pizza delivery man is glad that she does not scream (even though, at this hour, there is no one in the strip-mall who would hear).

Taking advantage of the relative calm, the pizza delivery man fetches a chair, sits down beside the good-looking manager (with her entire body gripped by a palsy), and starts detailing the union's demands and how far they are willing to go to satisfy these demands.

When the good-looking manager starts trembling, the pizza delivery man volunteers to return her earlier favor: "One second, I'm gonna get you a Coke."

Beside the soda-dispenser, he continues talking: "Come on, don't fucking wig-out on me – That's not your finger!"

From against the opposite counter-top where he has been watching, the Congolese "freedom fighter" saunters over to the pizza delivery man with the biggest shit-eating grin – Slinging his arm around the soda-dispenser, he takes a drag from his hash cigarette, exhaling through pursed, whistling lips: "That's not your finger?" - He laughs: "You are not an *Ilunga* at all, my friend – You are a fucking king today!"

3.

From 1885 to 1908, the territory that is now the Democratic Republic of the Congo belonged to the Congo Free State, a state privately owned and controlled by King Leopold II, King of the Belgians: A man who, like the pizza delivery man, was responsible for cutting off a few appendages.

In his book, *Freedom and Organization (1934),* Bertrand Russell had the following to say about Leopold's "administration" of his Congo Free State: His African fiefdom: His rubber-producing, African cash-cow:

> "Each village was ordered by the
> authorities to collect and bring in a
> certain amount of rubber -- as much as
> the men could bring in by neglecting
> all work for their own maintenance. If
> they failed to bring the required
> amount, their women were taken away
> and kept as hostages in compounds or
> in the harems of government
> employees. If this method failed,

native troops, many of them cannibals,
were sent into the village to spread
terror, if necessary by killing some of
the men; but in order to prevent a
waste of cartridges they were ordered
to bring one right hand for every
cartridge used. If they missed, or used
cartridges on game, they cut off the
hands of living persons to make up the
necessary number."

When the Congolese "freedom fighter"
proclaimed the pizza delivery man to be "a fucking
king today!" he did so because his referent for a
western monarch is the infamous King Leopold II –
For the Congolese "freedom fighter", the man who
cuts off another's appendage (be it a hand or a finger)
and uses it to intimidate is a king: God's authority on
earth.

4.

Romans 13:1-7:

[1] Everyone is to obey the governing
authorities, because there is no

authority except from God and so whatever authorities exist have been appointed by God. [2] So anyone who disobeys an authority is rebelling against God's ordinance; and rebels must expect to receive the condemnation they deserve. [3]Magistrates bring fear not to those who do good, but to those who do evil. So if you want to live with no fear of authority, live honestly and you will have its approval; [4] it is there to serve God for you and for your good. *But if you do wrong, then you may well be afraid; because it is not for nothing that the symbol of authority is the sword: it is there to serve God, too, as his avenger, to bring retribution to wrongdoers.* [5] You must be obedient, therefore, not only because of this retribution, but also for conscience's sake. [6] And this is why you should pay taxes, too, because the

authorities are all serving God as his
agents, even while they are busily
occupied with that particular task. [7]
Pay to each one what is due to each:
taxes to the one to whom tax is due,
tolls to the one to whom tolls are due,
respect to the one to whom respect is
due, honor to the one to whom honor
is due.

5.

With his arm still slung around the soda-
dispenser, the "freedom fighter" reminisces about the
Protestant missionaries who lived in his village – He
recalls one of his Sunday school lessons: "Everyone is
to obey the boss because there is no boss 'cept from
God. And anyone who fights against the boss? He
fights against God – And the man who fights against
God, he goes to hell."

As a former catechumen, the pizza delivery
man recognizes Romans 13 – For reminding him, he
wants to force shit past the "freedom fighter's" shit-
eating grin, down into his throat.

Trying to shake the dispiriting feelings elicited by the Congolese' vernacular recitation of scripture, the pizza delivery man focuses on getting the Coke ready for his new good-looking manager: "So what do you like? Half-and-half? – One part cola to one part ice?"

Shell-shocked; eyes still fixed on the severed-finger at the edge of her desk, the pizza delivery man's new manager says nothing.

To himself, he thinks, "Great – Way to be there for me, lady."

Uncharacteristically empathic; like he senses that he has been misunderstood, the "freedom fighter" reaches out to the obviously dejected pizza delivery man, placing a weather-beaten and calloused hand on his shoulder – Turning the pizza delivery man to face him; indifferent to the fact that he is mid-pour, the Congolese "freedom fighter" orders him to hold his head high: "Because you are a king now (the boss) and not a rebel – And you have made us right with God."

Overwhelmed; grateful because he believes the pizza delivery man has reconciled him with the Divine, the Congolese "freedom fighter" pulls him to his emaciated chest, tears streaming down his cheeks.

Watching the soda-dispenser empty its syrupy contents onto the pizzeria's slip-resistant flooring; unable to move, the pizza delivery man just stands there, mulling over a scriptural loophole that says unimportant men can violently rebel against God's authority on earth provided they are successful.

Wrapped in the Congolese' bear-hug, it takes the pizza delivery man some time before he puts two and two together, before he sees that because he is the new sword-wielding right hand of God (like Simon Peter at the arrest of Christ); that because he has become the boss of a small collective of delivery men and one good-looking manager, he has actually been successful in making himself into an important man.

Putting two and two together shatters the pizza delivery man.

It shatters him into a million pieces, like he were a cheap vase knocked from its display stand,

193

inexpressibly relieved because it never wanted to be made like that.

The simple math collapses him, breaking down his barriers and freeing him to return the embrace of the Congolese who cries for his own joy, "You're the fucking king, [Pizza delivery man]! – The fucking king!"

6.

The pungent, psychoactive smoke hanging like thick smog around the Congolese "freedom fighter" makes short work of the pizza delivery man's euphoria – It causes him extreme anxiety.

In his ear, he can hear the Devil say, "You two look like such fags right now, especially with a fine looking woman sitting right over there."

The pizza delivery man points out the fact that his good-looking manager is paralyzed with fear.

The Devil's expression indicates that he does not understand what that has to do with anything: "Whatever, man, you're the boss. Look, I'm just gonna jet – Glad I could be here to see this."

With his linear memory corrupted by potent, second-hand hashish; unable to tell what was exactly said and by whom, the pizza delivery man anxiously mutters, "Wait, I'm sorry – I didn't meant to call you a fag."

Still pressing the pizza delivery man to his chest, the "freedom fighter" strokes his hair and tries to soothe him: "Shhh, don't fight it, motherfucker – Deep breaths."

But the pizza delivery man does fight it – He wants to know where the Devil is going: "With my soul! – Where are you *jetting* to, you prick?"

The Devil slaps him on the shoulder ("[Pizza delivery man], you're so fucked-up right now; it's hilarious!") before he tells him that he does not have his soul: "When the fuck did you give it to me exactly? Did you slip it into my pocket when I wasn't looking?"

Fighting against his high, the pizza delivery man answers in a hushed voice, "No, jackass – When we killed our boss and chopped off his fingers."

The Devil smiles, like he had almost forgotten about that – He repeats himself, "I don't have your fucking soul."

To which, the stoned pizza delivery man nervously giggles: "Because I made us right with God, yeah?"

The Devil stares down the pizza delivery man like he had just insulted his life's work ("No, you didn't, queer-bait – I've met the Man Who did that."), gruffly adding, "I didn't make life in your apartment a living hell because I wanted your soul – I just wanted you to get your ass off the bean bag chair to keep the great big ball of human fucking up rolling along!"

Having said that, with all seriousness the Devil bows to the pizza delivery man ("Your Majesty."), and then walks out the rear-entrance of the pizzeria (leaving the door open) across to where there are no street-lights, disappearing from view.

7.

Out in the pizzeria's parking lot, the pizza delivery man's co-worker cannot contain himself – He wants to know what their new good-looking manager had to say about their demands.

The pizza delivery man relays the story of how he handled the situation ("Pretty fucking *debonair*, if that's the word.") and how he brought her around after she slipped into a catatonic state ("Coca-Cola fixes everything. You know the highway patrol uses it to clean up blood after accidents – Hell, if it can dissolve a penny, right?") – The pizza delivery man assures his co-worker and the new guy that their good-looking manager is very much under his thumb: "We've got nothing to worry about here – So, what's the word from the others?"

The pizza delivery man's co-worker does not answer because he has taken issue with what he has heard; he wants their good-looking manager to be under his thumb, too - The pizza delivery man reads this on his co-worker's face, but shelves addressing this real problem for later.

The new guy answers that he heard back from the pretty boy and the dry-heaver: "Both did exactly as we said: Brought the notes and the fingers to their managers and kept their fucking mouths shut."

The new guy emphasizes that he made sure of that: "So no one is getting hired or fired at their pizzerias without us giving the go-ahead."

The good news pleases the pizza delivery man – The dry night air feels cleaner and crisper.

He asks about the crybaby: "What's the score there?"

The new guy casts a troubled look over at the pizza delivery man's co-worker who answers for them: "He's fallen off the radar, man – We can't find him."

The pizza delivery man is surprised to have lost the crybaby: "Come on, it's not like the fat boy fell into a crack and disappeared."

Tossing his car keys into the air and catching them with a deftness that impresses himself, the pizza delivery man orders his co-worker and the new guy to find the "two junior members" of the union and reconvene back at his apartment to organize a search: "For Wee Willie Winkie running through the town."

Failing to hold himself back, the new guy blurts out, "What if he's gone to the cops, [Pizza delivery man]?"

The pizza delivery man considers his car key toss and, feeling lucky, answers that he seriously doubts that: "Do you think that little cunt-rag wants to go to prison? Get gang-raped? – [New guy], he knows we'll take him down with us."

Walking back to his car, the pizza delivery man shouts over his shoulder that he will see them all at his apartment in an hour.

8.

When the crybaby lunges from the backseat to stab him in the back of the head with a pair of scissors, the pizza delivery man has a panoply of thoughts and observations.

Observing the crybaby's berserker rage in his rearview mirror when he goes to adjust it, the pizza delivery man first thinks, "So that's why the car door was unlocked." – He then wonders why he did not take the scissors back from the fat little bastard after he had used them to cut his waistband ("I could've sworn...").

Staring into the reflection of the shrieking, doughy crybaby ("Wearing my fucking sweat pants!") with his gaping mouth, the pizza delivery man has the impression of looking down the barrel of a gun aimed at his skull – At this moment, the pizza delivery man would really like for the Congolese "freedom fighter" not to be passed out in the passenger seat, having gotten so lit in the pizzeria.

When he instinctively moves to avoid being stabbed, like a very amateur boxer avoiding a punch, the pizza delivery man catches a glimpse of something else in his rearview mirror, something else in the backseat of his car.

To his surprise, that something is the Devil.

Though caught in a life-and-death situation that requires absolute focus, the pizza delivery man now fights as much to understand why the Devil is back in his life ("I thought we squared shit when I got made.") and why he pats the crybaby on his fleshy bottom like a supportive parent.

When the first jab of the crybaby's scissors narrowly misses him, the pizza delivery man dives back in the opposite direction – He feels like a barge pilot trying to make an impossible turn.

The crybaby's sweaty reflection looks winded – The pizza delivery man hopes that there is not much left in him.

Apparently fearing as much, the Devil shouts words of encouragement: "Eyes on the prize, [Crybaby]! Just think of what the news ladies will say about you! – Brave son-of-a-bitch!"

Because the pizza delivery man has not forgotten the story of the little vendor that could, he cannot understand why the Devil is jerking the crybaby around just to kill him: "What the fuck, man? - You're doing this *now*?"

The Devil's response is to mime a masturbating hand while he stares lewdly into the pizza delivery man's own mirror image: "Don't even try to put that guilt on me, motherfucker - I did Gandhi."

While trying to understand what the Devil meant by that, something sharp hits the pizza delivery man of this "life-never-to-be-lived" in the back of the head.

9.

The police have to quickly cordon off the crime scene.

When word gets out ("Was it the bitch in the office?"), the media and the gawkers arrive en masse to push against each other, elbowing one another for a better view – Thronged together, they bulge against the police line, like an expanding belly that threatens to burst and make a hell of a mess.

Because of the crowd, it is a while before the cops decide to move "Madame Bardot".

When she is led hand-cuffed from the motel room to the awaiting police vehicle in the parking lot, she wears her own clothes: A revealing dress that drives the guys watching on the roof of the liquor store to whistle and cat call.

Spectators on the ground nearest the police line crane their heads backwards to laugh and poke fun at the saucy young men.

For the attention, "Madame Bardot" smiles a practiced naïve smile – For which she is rewarded by a man shouting from within the jumble of onlookers that he will wait for her: "I love you, [Madame Bardot]!"

When her vehicle drives away, the crowds disperse (either to go home and share the news with friends and family, or to follow her and her police escort).

By the time the medical examiners wheel the pizza delivery man's body out of the motel room to load it onto the ambulance, only a few people remain (among them is Robin Fletcher – He has not moved from the curb on the opposite side of the street since he lost his photographs and his mind).

Having recovered a little of his mind (enough with which to torment himself), Fletcher glowers at the pizza delivery man with his black body bag and his collapsible red stretcher; and, like a homeless man

sick in the head, loudly curses him for not being
Heath Ledger: "So you aren't any fucking good to me,
you worthless dead fuck!"